The Delta Factor

..ET Thrillers by Mickey Spillane

(0451)

☐	THE BIG KILL	(134346—$2.95)*
☐	BLOODY SUNRISE	(120507—$2.25)
☐	THE BODY LOVERS	(127951—$2.50)*
☐	THE BY-PASS CONTROL	(092260—$1.75)
☐	THE DAY OF THE GUNS	(129857—$2.50)*
☐	THE DEATH DEALERS	(129849—$2.50)*
☐	THE DEEP	(121031—$2.50)
☐	THE DELTA FACTOR	(122089—$2.50)
☐	THE ERECTION SET	(131452—$3.50)*
☐	THE GIRL HUNTERS	(129830—$2.50)*
☐	I, THE JURY	(113969—$2.95)
☐	KILLER MINE	(117972—$1.50)
☐	THE LAST COP OUT	(119053—$2.50)
☐	THE LONG WAIT	(121902—$2.50)
☐	ME, HOOD	(116798—$1.95)
☐	MY GUN IS QUICK	(097912—$1.95)
☐	ONE LONELY NIGHT	(121651—$2.50)
☐	THE SNAKE	(122091—$2.50)
☐	SURVIVAL ... ZERO	(121058—$2.50)
☐	THE TOUGH GUYS	(092252—$1.75)
☐	THE TWISTED THING	(122070—$2.50)
☐	VENGEANCE IS MINE	(132645—$2.50)*

*Prices slightly higher in Canada

MICKEY SPILLANE

The Delta
Factor

A SIGNET BOOK

NEW AMERICAN LIBRARY

PUBLISHER'S NOTE

This novel is a work of fiction. Names, characters, places, and incidents are either the product of the author's imagination or are used fictitiously, and any resemblance to actual persons, living or dead, events, or locales is entirely coincidental.

SIGNET, SIGNET CLASSIC, MENTOR, PLUME, MERIDIAN AND NAL BOOKS *are published by New American Library, 1633 Broadway, New York, New York 10019*

FIRST SIGNET PRINTING, FEBRUARY, 1968

11   12   13   14   15   16   17   18   19

PRINTED IN THE UNITED STATES OF AMERICA

For Ward . . .

1

THE LIGHT HAD a strange pattern to it, striped horizontally and tinted with a pinkish glow. There was something unreal about it, like opening your eyes under water and looking up toward the sky. It rippled and swam, hypnotically out of focus, giving it an eerie dream-quality. Even the subdued sounds that rode on its current were distorted and out of reach until one particular one took shape gradually and I recognized it as *Morgan*. Then I let my eyes slit open a little further and the light pattern emerged as venetian blinds across the white-walled room from the bed and the sounds those of voices in quiet, cold argument.

I knew, then.

Hell, *they* couldn't have reached me. The police, the great agencies subsidized in the government budget, private experts intrigued by the reward . . . none of them even came near me. It took a punk kid in a stolen heap being chased by a squad car to smash me through a store window, and an overzealous intern who didn't like unidentified accident cases and submitted fingerprint samples to the local precinct house to nail me.

Now they were fighting it out over who had custody over Morgan the Raider, and Morgan the Raider was me.

For a while I just lay there listening, grinning inside, but not letting it show on my face. That would have hurt anyway. I watched them through an aperture of my eyelids as narrow as possible, enjoying their performance as the sensation of living gradually oozed back into my body. When it reached my arm I felt the bite of metal around my wrist, put a gentle pressure against it that met with solid resistance and stifled another grin again because they were afraid of taking any chances at all this time.

The doctor's voice held a restrained anger. He said, "You can keep security around this room without shackling him to the bed, Mr. Rice. This is the fifth floor, the windows are barred, a policeman's outside and my patient isn't in any condition to move. Not just yet."

Boredom comes early to accomplished cops. Explanations to civilian types become patient, paternal and positive. "This isn't just a patient, Doctor. This is Morgan."

"I know who he is. I found him for you, didn't I?"

"Yes. You'll get an official departmental commendation for it. I believe there's a considerable reward involved too."

"Screw your reward, Mr. Rice. I want my patient unmolested."

"I'm sorry, Doctor."

The white-coated medic seemed to move purposely. "I can force your hand if I have to."

"Not this time."

"This time," he said deliberately.

"Why make trouble?" the cop asked him. "I can pull strings too. Look . . . let me put it to you again. This man is dangerous. He isn't like an ordinary hood with behavior patterns we're used to. We could deal with that. He's not part of any antisocial group our people could classify and work against in a logical manner. His type comes out of another era entirely. By today's standards we can't even define him. Do you know what they call him?"

For a few seconds there was silence, then the doctor said, "Morgan the Raider."

"Do you know why?"

"No."

"Do you remember another Morgan?"

"Only the pirate."

Like a parent pleased with his child's correct answer, the cop said pleasantly, "Exactly, Doctor. In his own way, he's a pirate too. You didn't fight pirates with police techniques. It took navies and armies to wipe them out. They were a peculiar breed given to command, who drew unequaled respect from their subordinates, lived by their own rules until they were almost a government unto themselves, reaped fantastic wealth and terrified half the world." He paused, then added, "He's like that."

The doctor crossed to the window and opened the blinds a little further. "Since you're getting so historical, Mr. Rice, I'd better remind you that you're forgetting something."

"Oh?"

"Some of those they called pirates were privateers authorized by one government to prey on another. They held letters of marque from their governments and in their own countries were held in highest esteem."

I knew the cop was smiling. I couldn't see his face, but I knew he was. "Exactly my point, Doctor," he said. "That is what we're afraid of. An ordinary criminal type doesn't plan and execute a forty-million-dollar robbery. He doesn't have the tolerance to withstand all the efforts that go into making him reveal where he disposed of a haul of that size. He doesn't have the aptitude to escape from a solitary-confinement cell in a maximum-security prison and stay at large three years."

The cop leaned back in his chair and said, "Let's say he *could* have been acting as a privateer, Doctor. Let an enemy government loose enough of them in this country and the destruction they could cause would be immense."

Silently, my mouth formed the words "You stupid bastard."

Very slowly, the doctor turned around and walked up beside me. I let my eyes close and shut him out. He said, "That's an assumption, isn't it?"

"In these days we have to work on assumptions quite often. You *are* familiar with the details of the case, aren't you?"

"I know what the papers said. It was a shipment of currency from the Washington mint to New York, wasn't it?"

"Forty million dollars' worth in common bills. The paper volume would fill a medium-sized truck."

"You people don't take very good care of the public's cash."

"It was well guarded."

The doctor's voice had a laugh in it. "Was it?"

Rice said nothing for a moment, then when he spoke there was an edge in his words. "The aggressor always has the advantage."

"Don't excuse your own mistakes, Mr. Rice. You caught him once."

"With twelve thousand dollars of recorded bills in his possession. He never had a chance to spend any of it."

"If I remember right, that was an accident too."

Rice let out a little chuckle. "You'd be surprised how often accidents, as you put it, pay off. The rooming house where he boarded was raided by Treasury agents looking for narcotics held by another tenant and they turned up his cache. We killed two birds with one stone."

"Commendable. Why didn't you keep him?"

"Maybe now we'll learn how he broke out. If he could do it there, this place would be a cream puff, so the cuffs stay on him, Doctor."

"Unless it interferes with his treatment, Mr. Rice. Don't forget that."

I opened my eyes and looked up at the medic. He was watching me with peculiar curiosity, seeing both a patient and a specimen, but his expression had a determined set to it that no police agency was going to intimidate. I said, "You tell him, Doc."

Rice's chair scraped the floor quickly and a blurred figure of a blocky man in a gray suit drifted into my line of vision, but only for a moment. It was all just a little too tiresome and I drifted back slowly into the pleasant void of sleep where there weren't any aches or pains and the dreams all had nice, creamy-skinned women in them.

The netherworld is only a vacation from reality. It never lasts long enough. Waking up was a jarring thing because it happened so abruptly; every detail of the situation clear with total recall. There was no pain any more, simply a muscular soreness and a skin prickling where the stiches were still tight, but I had had that sensation so often it didn't bother me at all. My left arm was still tethered to the bed frame, loosely enough to allow limited movement, but a complete restraint to anything further.

There were three of them in the room now, each earmarked with the odd composure that gets ground into the makeup of professional cops. Rice was there, the Washington representative who worked under the C.I.A.; Carter, the Treasury Department's troubleshooter; and a big, solid-looking guy in a rumpled suit that bulged over a gun in a belt holster who was N.Y.P.D. all the way. He didn't appreciate anyone infringing on his jurisdiction and looked it. Someone had given him orders and he took them, but he didn't have to like it. When the doctor came in the cop was introduced briefly as Inspector Jack Doherty and I pegged him as the big one the mayor appointed to work directly out of the D.A.'s office on special assignment.

Man, they were sure giving me top-quality treatment.

It was the doctor who saw me wide awake first. His mouth twisted in a funny little grin when he said, "Excuse me, gentlemen," then he came over to me, felt my pulse automatically, raised one lid with a thumb and peered at my eye and asked, "How do you feel?"

"Like forty million," I told him.

"Think you'll get to spend it?"

I grinned back at him. "Nobody else will, that's for sure. They pay off that reward yet?"

"You heard what I told Rice, didn't you?"

"Sure, but did you mean it?"

"Well, I haven't bought any Cadillacs lately."

"You'll get it."

"I expect to. Ten years after I hang out my shingle."

"That's doing it the hard way."

"And that's the way it's going to be," he told me. "Any soreness?"

"Some. How do I look?"

He shrugged and dropped my hand. "Minor concussion, cuts and abrasions, two broken ribs. We were afraid of internal injuries, but apparently there weren't any. You were lucky, Morgan."

"Yeah, I sure was," I laughed. "When am I to be released?"

"Depending upon your own complaint, anytime. You can delay it for a few days if you feel like it."

"Hell, why bother?"

"Every day's a day. I hear the chow's better here than in a cell."

"I haven't tasted any of it yet," I said. "At least there they don't feed you through a tube and they let you up long enough to go to the john. I don't go this bedpan routine."

"Take your pick. It's a hell of a choice for a millionaire, though."

"Isn't it, though?"

The other three moved in, standing there until the doctor finished, watching me like a bug on a pin. When the doctor stepped back Rice leaned forward and said, "Well?"

"Anytime, buddy," I told him. "Make it easy on yourselves."

For some reason the three of them looked at each other, annoyance scratching furrows at the corners of their eyes. Inspector Doherty seemed to clamp his teeth together like he wanted to swing at me and Carter made a tight-lippd scowl as if he had bitten into something distasteful.

Only Rice was impassive. He stared at me, his eyes never leaving mine, and said in almost a whisper, "Stay loose, Morgan. It's not over. It's just beginning and you'll be back where you came from or else you'll be dead. Luck

can ride either side of the table, but just remember that
you can never beat the house odds."

The building as an innocuous affair, a second-story
apartment over a deserted grocery in a block condemned
by the city for an urban renewal project. The truck they
had used for transportation was a Department of Public
Works vehicle no different from two others parked nearby
and if anyone was curious enough to look, we were just
some of the city planning board inspecting the properties.

But it was a lot more than that. Only Inspector Doherty
and his plainclothes assistant were on New York's payroll.
The rest came from the massive complex on the Potomac
and acted with the strange reserve of a meeting of the
Joint Chiefs of Staff. It was an appraisal that wasn't far
off. Each of them was the head of an agency directly responsible to the White House and if a decision or an action backfired, they carried their heads in their hands.

I kept getting those surreptitious glances of distaste
from the time they outfitted me in new clothes until they
sat me at a corner of the table in the dust-filled room,
enough out of line with the others so that I would know
that I wasn't one of them, but something dirty yet necessary, like a squeamish woman putting a slimy worm on a
hook just to catch a nice clean fish.

There were no introductions, but then, I didn't need
any. Gavin Woolart, the ace from the State Department,
was running the show. He didn't appreciate the look of recognition I gave his associates in the beginning, but was
shrewd enough to realize my profession called for intimate
knowledge of people. All people. He was smart enough to
stay away from the antagonistic angles even if it hurt and
when he was ready he addressed me so damn formally it
was funny.

Hell, he could have called me by my number. Not by
my first name, though. I didn't have any.

Instead, he said, "Mr. Morgan, you are probably wondering what this is all about."

I couldn't resist the invitation. "Mr. Woolart, that is one
bitch of a statement. So . . . yes, I *am* wondering what
this is all about. I'm a convicted criminal, an escapee and
here I am in a new suit of clothes surrounded by V.I.P.'s
with sour looks. If you had asked me I'd say it was a new
slant in trying to retrieve your forty million bucks."

Somebody coughed and Woolart glared at him. "Let's
forget that for the moment."

"Thanks a bunch," I said.

"How much time did you draw?"

I shrugged. They knew the answer. "Thirty years. Nothing was concurrent so they'll pick me up on the other charges as soon as I use up the time." I grinned at him. "*If* I use up the time."

"Please don't try to be comical," he said.

"What have I got to lose?"

"Some of those thirty years, for one thing."

I didn't get it at all. I leaned forward and leaned on the table. Something was about to get mighty interesting. "Let's put it this way then," I said. "What have I got to gain?"

Once more, there was an exchange of glances around the room. Woolart tapped the tip of a pencil on the tabletop and the sound was like that of a clock about to run out. If somebody didn't wind it it would stop.

Gavin Woolart pressed down on the pencil and the point broke. It was an effectual little gesture. "Let *me* put it *this* way, Mr. Morgan. We know your status. We are fully acquainted with your background from the day you were born, through college, your wartime service to the present. Nothing has been omitted. An intensive investigation of your past has resulted in a dossier that details every facet of your life."

"Except one thing, apparently," I said. My voice was tight and husky and I could hardly get the words out.

"Yes."

"Now I'll ask it. What?"

"Your potential."

I didn't like the feeling I got. It started at the back of my neck like a cold breeze and made the muscles in my shoulders bunch up into knots. They didn't even want to know where the forty million went to, so whatever it was put my neck on the line. The big *No* was already there inside my mouth to say but I couldn't do it until he had laid it out and I could hardly wait until he did.

"Curious, Mr. Morgan?"

"Not especially," I lied.

"You should be. With your next stay in the penitentiary, security will be absolute maximum."

"That won't help."

Woolart let a little smile play with his mouth. "That's what I mean, Mr. Morgan."

I shook my head, not understanding.

"Your potential," he said. "You seem to have something nobody else has. A strange talent indeed. You do things of

major importance, then reinforce them by another action.
It's too bad your abilities weren't directed into normal
channels."

"For me it was normal."

"Again, Mr. Morgan, that's what I'm referring to."

I half stood up. "Damn it, get to the point. I don't like
being held like this. You know what a lawyer would do in
court when I told him what you pulled?"

"Nothing, Mr. Morgan," Woolart said quietly. "You
have been convicted, you have escaped, and now you're
being recaptured. Legally, I think he'd advise you to shut
up and listen."

I sat down. Like I said before, I really didn't have anything to lose. Not one damn thing at all.

Woolart glanced around the room, then out of habit
opened an attaché case in front of him. It wasn't necessary. He knew every word that was written there by heart,
but it was a habit he couldn't break. When he had the
papers aligned to his satisfaction he said, "This offer is
being made against our judgment, Mr. Morgan. It was
suggested by an authority higher than ours, so we have to
make it. However, we stipulated that if it is refused upon
its initial presentation, then it never will be made again.
Frankly, I am hoping that you will refuse it. Everything
will be much simpler then and we can proceed in the matter normally. But as I said, this choice is not ours."

I could feel their eyes on me. They weren't looking . . .
they were watching. Not one of them felt differently from
Woolart and the expectation was there, clear and strong,
that my answer would be negative. Anything else would be
one of stupidity and they weren't giving me credit for that.

"Say it," I told him.

He shuffled the papers a moment, then looked up at me.
"It regards the value you put on your life. Whether you
prefer to spend it inside a prison until there's nothing left
of you except the remnants of a man or take a chance on
losing it altogether with the possible alternative of only
spending a portion of your sentence behind bars with at
least a few years of active, enjoyable life left to you." He
stopped and ran his tongue around the inside of his
mouth. "It isn't very much of a choice, is it?"

"You haven't spelled it all the way out either, Mr. Woolart."

"Since you'll never be in a position to transmit any of
this information . . . even if it is speculative . . . to any-

one else, I'll go a little further, but let me put it in hypothetical fashion at any rate."

I waved my hand disgustedly. I didn't like it at all. "Be my guest."

"There is a certain country," he said, "neighboring . . . apparently friendly as long as they receive our largesse, but in reality, closer politically to those we consider an enemy of this country. In their prison they have a person our scientific circles need desperately in order to . . . ah . . . over come certain . . . ah . . . enemy advancements.

"We can not go in and liberate this person Again, frankly, we have tried and failed. In this age of propaganda and internal unrest, the United States cannot put itself in an unfavorable position. This one country is using this person as a pawn, ready to move in either direction, looking for favors from both sides. The unfortunate part is, that the person involved is of advanced age and not expected to live too much longer. It is imperative that we have the information he can give us before it is too late. One aspect is this: if he is already dead, this other country can conceal that fact and still extract . . . well, tribute, from our government for any length of time."

This time Gavin Woolart stopped his incessant handling of the papers and looked directly at me. "We need two things," he said. "One, if he *is* dead, knowledge of the fact."

"And?" I put in.

"The second . . . if he *is* alive, we need *him*. And that, Mr. Morgan, is where your potential comes in."

I knew what he was going to say. I could almost smell it.

"This is the proposition . . . that you go into that country, commit a crime of our specifications that will get you sentenced to that prison, then effect an escape with either the information of his death or the person himself. For this action the government will take into consideration our recommendation of a reduced sentence for your prior, ah, activities and it will be acted upon."

"All this in writing, I suppose," I grinned.

"Nothing in writing." He didn't grin at all.

"Come on, buddy. I made deals like that during the war. Give me a witness that will stay alive, at least."

"Nothing."

"Balls," I said. "You're like the insurance companies these days. You get paid for taking chances, but you sure don't want to take any." I leaned back in my chair. "Little man, I'd sooner take my chances on getting out of your damn pen. That I can do and the odds are even better."

Gavin Woolart's face flushed a deep red with controlled anger. His smile was friendly, but his lips were almost bloodless. "No other deal," he grimaced.

I never expected it, but it happened anyway. That deep, resonant voice of Inspector Doherty's cut through the room like a knife through toilet paper and he said, "I witnessed it, Morgan. Do what you want."

Two of them came out of their chairs like they had been shot. Carter swung around, anger contorting his face. "Listen, Inspector . . ."

Jack Doherty had been around just a little too long. Nobody impressed him any more. He had pounded too many beats, seen too much action, worked with too many administrations to get cut off by somebody outside his own domain. He was totally impassive, sitting there like a fight-scarred tiger, too lazy and too competent to be bothered wasting his talents on the young bucks looking for a slice of his harem when all he had to do was growl to buzz them off. He said, "I don't give a damn for this bum one way or another. I've made deals with bums and politicians alike and stuck with them, but never one that was raw. This one stinks. So you're in a bind and now it's your turn. It's still my territory and keep it in your heads. All you have to do is nod and he goes back in, but don't play around with his life. He didn't knock anybody off you know of. I'll be a witness to this deal whether you like it or not."

"Thanks, Inspector," I told him.

"Don't thank me, Morgan. Either way, you're still a loser in my book."

Carter and Woolart sat down slowly. "You haven't heard the last of this, Doherty," Carter told him.

The big cop made a gesture with his shoulders. "So sue me," he said and took a drag on his cigar.

Woolart looked at me. "Well?"

"Supposing I get to this hypothetical country and decide to cut out?"

Bluntly, Woolart said, "An agent will accompany you. Others will be on hand. In that event you will be eliminated. This is one of the simpler phases of the operation."

"Uh-huh." I folded my hands and studied him again. "You're appealing to something, Woolart."

No mister this time.

"It can't be to my consideration of a shorter term behind bars," I said. "Funny enough, life in any state is better than none at all. It can't be to what you consider my sense of adventure because the reward factor is too small. So what is it?"

"Neither, Morgan." *And he didn't say mister either.* "I have no consideration in the matter at all. I told you it came from higher up. Maybe it's an appeal to your patriotism."

"Then they'll have to do better than that."

All the eyes made the rounds of the other eyes at the table again. This time it was Carter who said, "What are you thinking of, Mr. Morgan?"

At least he kept the mister in.

"Maybe they don't want the forty million back," I said.

Seconds pass slowly when nobody wants to commit themselves. Only Doherty was grinning because he liked binds himself and he didn't have anything outside a professional affection for the rest.

"We're not at liberty to decide on that matter," Woolart said quietly.

I had them then. "Like hell you're not. This was dropped in your laps and you were told to handle it. You were told to make the deal and if you come back empty-handed somebody will drop a hot potato in them. Buddies, you done bought the farm. Now I'll lay it out. If I pull it off, you knock off fifteen years, all sentences to run concurrently, and nobody touches that loot. Plain enough?"

"No." Gavin Woolart's tone was adamant.

"Is your boy worth forty million, Mr. Woolart? Can you do the job yourself?"

And from the rear Carter said, "Let it stand, Gavin. It's the only deal we can make."

For a few long seconds Woolart just stared at me. It was his kind of game, this mental cat-and-mouse bit, and he had been at it a long time where all the participants were experts. Now he was calling on all his resources to catalog me properly. Then, very quietly, he said, "No."

"Why, Gavin?" Carter asked him. The rest of the room was very quiet.

I said, "He's considering a possibility, Mr. Carter. A forty-million-dollar possibility. He hates to see that kind of money cut from the budget. Now let me inject another possibility . . . that I didn't take it. Oh, sure, it was proven in court through circumstantial evidence, but more than one innocent person went that route before me. The cute little possibility he's considering is that if you guarantee I can keep the forty big ones . . . and I didn't heist it to begin with . . . but manage to get my hands on it in the meantime, you people are up the creek. Make it a public issue and some of our more progressive papers will take you apart . . . not to say what will happen politically. Right, Woolart?"

He didn't answer me.

I said, "He knows I might pull it off, too." I let a grin crease my face and relaxed in the chair. "It's an interesting challenge."

Gavin Woolart's face was drawn into a tight mask. "There's no doubt about your having that money, Morgan."

"Or that I might get it," I added.

He shrugged, not changing his expression. "Either way, the answer is still No."

"You authorized to make the decision or does it go through channels, Mr. Woolart?"

He didn't have to give me the answer. I saw the sudden narrowing of his eyes. "For your own satisfaction, you'll get an opinion from higher quarters, but I can assure you it will be negative. However, there's a time element involved and I advise you not to delay making up your mind or the entire situation will revert unconditionally to your recapture."

"But the rest of the deal stands?"

"That's the offer. Take your choice."

I nodded. "Okay, buddy, I'll take it." I scanned the room and watched the small glances they exchanged, those tiny motions of relief like finding out that there was still some time left in the ball game after all. I said, "How do you know you can trust me?"

Gavin Woolart gathered his papers together and stood up. His eyes were cold beads that said he hated every facet of the arrangement, but it was out of his hands. Very tersely, he told me, "We don't, Morgan."

2

FOR A WEEK they sweated me in the Montebahn Hotel, a crappy six-story building wedged between two similar ones in the upper forties. Maybe it was to condition me to the idea of what they wanted. Maybe it was to diagram the security arrangements they could use if they wanted to.

They had recruited types from somewhere who seemed just too damned innocuous to be carrying a badge until you spotted all the little things that marked them as being top guns who would as soon slice you up as say hello. The rooms opposite and flanking mine each held a pair, with each door cracked enough so they could see any passing movement in the hall outside. Nobody had to tell me there would be others. Every exit from the roof to the basement would be covered with a twenty-four-hour watch after a lot of heavy minds went into screening any possible escape route.

A half hour after I was in the room I spotted a couple of bugs they had planted but didn't try to scramble them. In this age of electronics they didn't need anything quite so obvious, so my guess was that they were deliberately left exposed enough to see what action I'd take. The mirror over the battered dresser was new enough to be a giveway. The Montebahn Hotel didn't go to such extremes to make its guests happy, so the thing had to be a two-way job. The only amusement I had for a while was making faces into it, so if there was a psychiatrist back there trying to observe my actions for a possible stability factor, he was going to have a hell of a lot of notes to play with.

Oh, they were covering every angle, all right. The bathroom mirror was gimmicked the same way and that particular invasion of privacy I didn't like at all.

So I had to teach them a lesson. And like the man said . . . the aggressor always has the initial advantage.

The first night I shut the venetian blinds, pulled the musty curtains across the windows and got into bed in total darkness. I gave myself another hour, then pulled the drawer out from the nightstand beside the bed, hauled it under the covers and bashed the back out of it with the heel of my hand, then put it back in position. Any sound they heard would have been interpreted as a normal sleeper's movements and disregarded. And that was their tough luck.

Now all I could hope for was a habit pattern. I knew they were observing mine, so I could take advantage of theirs. The one thing they allowed me was room service from the grill downstairs and calling for a steak each night could damn near be expected. Something else could be expected too. In a place like this the steaks had to be tough, so the knife they supplied had to be sharp enough to compensate for it.

Then I began toilet training the great Federal agencies. Ten minutes after I finished I turned the news up on TV, went to the bathroom, draped a towel over the mirror there, knowing damn well they'd grin at my reluctance to be observed at what was my private affair, then I'd start to carve out the gun. Ten minutes was all I gave myself, then I flushed down the chips, shoved the chunk of wood well under the bathtub, went back and finished my coffee and called the waiter up to get the mess out of my room.

He was another one of them and his eyes neatly tabulated the dishes, the cutlery and everything else, then satisfied, he left. In the morning I'd use the john again properly so if they thought about it at all, I was just one of those regular types who never had any congestion of the lower tract.

The seventh day the flat little imitation automatic was finished. The only deviation from my habit pattern, and one they didn't notice, was that when I used the bathroom this time I took the bottle of Worchestershire sauce with me and it made a handy dye to blacken the wood of the mock-up gun. When I got back the gimmick was stuck inside my shirt, the bottle replaced and I called for the waiter again.

It had to figure out. They'd give me credit for having spotted the waiter, so they wouldn't take a chance of having me jump him and grab his rod, so he'd be unarmed. The door was always locked from the outside; the only time it was opened was when room service or the maid opened it. The maid was a scared hotel employee, so somebody would be waiting outside if I tried a break for it then. But when the waiter was there, the guard wouldn't be quite so worried.

He came in on schedule, but used to his job now, a little more efficient and unconcerned. I had arranged his habit pattern too. When he was pushing the tray toward the door I crossed behind him, ostensibly to adjust the TV, whipped the Worcestershire sauce bottle from the table and laid it across his ear from the only position the two-way mirror couldn't cover.

I was out the door with the wooden gun in my hand and the single guy there who turned around languidly expecting the waiter almost choked on his own spit and before instinct could make him react I shook my head and said, "Don't try it, old buddy. Just turn around."

It was all too fast. He did as I told him to. I fingered his gun from the belt holster, then pushed him toward the door of the room opposite mine. The other one inside got the same stricken look too. Without being told he went palms out on the tabletop he was playing cards on and let me take his gun too and all he did was look up at his partner and whisper hoarsely, "How the hell did it happen?"

"He had a gun," his partner told him.

"But . . . where?"

"Shut up," I said.

I used their own handcuffs around the radiator to keep them in place, gagged them both, tied their feet down with sheets so they couldn't bang around too much, then blew them a good-night kiss. They were two pretty sad-looking characters right then. Tomorrow they were going to be a lot sadder like a lot of others.

Just as long as one of them wasn't me, that was all right.

The rest was easy.

The elevator operator took me downstairs to the base-ment, after I pocketed his gun, held still while I tied and gagged him with his own clothes; the guy on the back exit did the same; the one roaming the small courtyard almost threw up with disgust, but submitted to the same procedure; then I was on my own. I was carrying a damn arsenal by then I didn't want or need, so I piled up the weaponry beside the last one, laid my wooden model on top for an object lesson and took off over the fence.

This time I let *them* sweat for a week. I let them get it all out of their systems, knowing damn well what was going on behind a lot of closed doors, and every time I thought about it I'd start to grin, then break out into a laugh, and more than once people thought I was a little nuts or else they would grin back figuring I was nursing a secret joke.

But the week was working for them too and I didn't realize it. Life gets too grim without its little challenges and they had thrown a big one at me. I made them eat it, but the big one I hadn't bought yet and the thought of it became more interesting every day.

After six days I had enough. On Saturday I went back to the Montebahn Hotel, asked the startled clerk for the same room I had occupied the week before, went up and turned on the TV, flopped on the bed and waited for the clerk to call the boys.

It was one hell of a boy, all right. They don't hardly make 'em like that any more. This agent was one of the loveliest women I had ever seen and if they had wanted a deterrent to an escape in the first place they should have sent her along earlier. Her hair was long and dark, sun-streaked in spots and tumbled around her shoulders in a carefully casual manner that almost made you stop looking at the rest of her. Except that was impossible. She never would have modeled for the women's fashion magazines because there was too lovely much of her, but from a man's point of view she was geometrical perfection. Even though she was agency trained, she didn't try to conceal the full rise of her breasts, or the sweep of waist to hips and the concave tautness of her belly. But for that matter, she couldn't. Like I said, there was just too lovely much of her. Her face was large dark eyes with a near-Oriental cast and a full-lipped mouth that had a damp sparkle, curved in a small, wry smile that studied me for a moment before she sat down.

"Kimberly Stacy," she said. "B-4 Intelligence, Section A. So you're the monster."

"Damn!" was all I could manage.

She smiled a little bigger this time. "You embarrassed a lot of my colleagues, Morgan."

"That's why they didn't come themselves."

"No . . . they simply thought it would be a little less conspicuous this way. Why did you do it?"

I squirmed up on the bed and stared at her. "Because I don't like people trying to outthink me. They needed a damn lesson . . ."

"No," she interrupted, "I didn't mean that. Why did you come back?"

My mouth twitched back into a grin. "Things were getting dull. I was having fun. I hated to see it stop."

She nodded as if she understood completely. "And when they stop being fun?"

I shrugged. "Then I'll do something else."

"You have only two choices," she reminded me.

"Do I?"

"It's a stop-action order now. You'll be killed if you try it again. The rest are waiting. Nobody's taking any chances this time."

"Why did they sweat me for a week, kid?"

"They were getting things organized. They didn't want any attention brought to this matter."

"Be candid, sugar," I said. "They had things organized before that."

Her mouth opened in a quiet laugh and I could see the even edges of her teeth. "I think they were testing you. They put you under maximum security and wanted to see what you'd do. Apparently they didn't think it could be done. You've compounded their embarrassment by coming back. They won't try that routine again."

"So?"

"Now you'll go with me. Quietly, no fuss, no bother and we'll help you make that decision."

"And if I don't?"

Her eyes twinkled at me. "I'll have to hold your hand," she said.

I let the laugh rumble out of my chest. "Okay, baby, after a threat like that I'm totally demoralized. There's only one thing."

"What's that?"

"Hold my hand. You'll be safer that way too."

"Don't be so sure of yourself, Morgan," she said. She meant it, too.

Something had changed in their faces. The aggressiveness was still there but a subtle respect had wiped out the antagonism. Only Jack Doherty remained untouched. The big cop still clamped a stub of a cigar in his teeth looking like he had eaten something sour, and eyed me impassively with no show of curiosity whatsoever.

Kimberly sat beside me and only then did I let go of her hand. We had left the others downstairs, the ones who had surrounded us on the street and squeezed into taxis fore and aft of our own. They had been a different bunch, their eyes frankly appraising me, hoping I would try something while their shift was on duty and looking disappointed when I didn't.

Gavin Woolart took the seat at the head of the table and went through his paper-shuffling routine again. He'd have to break that habit or somebody would make something of it someday. Finally he said, "That was a very ingenious ruse you pulled, Mr. Morgan."

I shrugged it off. "My pleasure. Maybe it'll keep your boys on their toes the next time."

"There won't be a next time."

"That's what you said the last time."

A flush of red crept into his face from his neckline. "There is one question . . . why you returned."

I saw Kim's head turn my way a fraction of a second and knew she was smiling. "I was bored," I told him.

"No other reason?"

"What one could there be?"

"We were hoping it was more an act of patriotism."

"Balls," I said.

Somebody coughed. Carter, from the Treasury Department, said, "You are at your best when you're bored, I assume?"

"I've never tried it any other way."

"Then I hope we're not making a mistake."

"What's that supposed to mean?"

For some reason they all turned and gave each other the briefest of glances. "We'll get to that later," he told me. "Now, Mr. Gavin . . . ?"

Gavin Woolart nodded and cleared his throat. "Your return, I take it, means you'll accept the terms of our . . . ah, proposal."

"Sure," I said.

"Then let us proceed directly to the heart of the matter. Time is an important element. We can't afford to waste any of it. Every day, every hour impairs our national security that much more. We have a lot of briefing for you."

"I'm a quick study, kid. Don't *you* waste time with non-essentials."

The red came back in his face again and he nodded. "Tell me, Morgan, have you ever heard of the Rose Castle?"

Tiny hairs on the back of my neck stood up and prickled my skin.

Yes, I knew the Rose Castle. At least I knew of it from a few who had been there and gotten out, a granite fortress built by the Spaniards in 1620, dedicated to death

*and destruction and used as a prison for political prisoners
with a reputation of being absolutely impregnable and to
tally escape-proof. The Spaniards hadn't fooled around
with modern conceptions of humane treatment for its in-
habitants.*

"So that's where he is," I said. "Yes, I know of it."

Woolart studied my face and said pleasantly, "Yes, I
can see that you have." He paused, then, "Does the name
Victor Sable mean anything to you?"

"No."

"It shouldn't. He is the one we want." From the pile of
papers he took three photographs and passed them down
the line to me. They were front and profile shots of a man
apparently in his sixties. He was partially bald, graying,
his expression a curious mixture of seriousness and stu-
diousness, and one I'd label as harmless. But for some reason he was pretty damn important.

"Background?"

"Nothing you need concern yourself with, Morgan."
From the papers he took several more and let me have
them. "Detailed sketches of the Rose Castle as complete as
we were able to get them. The top one is the original construction design we got from the archives in Madrid; the
others contain modifications supplied by certain former inmates and a few bribed ex-guards. However, there has
been some construction on modification of the interior
which we can't supply at this time."

I took the diagrams and glanced at them. It took only a
second to realize that an expert had laid out this crib.
They were asking the impossible when they wanted a mul-
tiple break out of the joint. I handed them back but Woolart waved me off. "Keep them to study, Morgan."

I grinned at him. "I already did, Woolart. I could duplicate them from memory right now."

For the first time Mr. Rice spoke: "I hope you aren't
being facetious, Mr. Morgan."

"It's my life, friend; I hope not."

"This isn't a conventional operation. We don't want to
leave anything to chance."

"Neither do I. Want me to show you my little memory
trick?"

I was annoyed and they knew it. Treasury's Carter said,
"All right, Morgan. We'll have to accept it."

"Then get on with it."

Woolart went through some more reshuffling before he
looked up. "We're basing your presence in that country on

the fact that you are a fugitive from justice. They know of
your forty-million-dollar coup and have always been willing to accept wealthy fugitives for as long as they could
pay for the pleasure. There is no extradition act in effect
between their country and ours, so whoever reaches their
shores is safe . . . for a while anyway, that is."

My mouth twisted in a funny grin. "They'll be expecting me to pay for the privilege then. I'll need financial
backing."

"Morgan . . ." Rice looked like he wanted to throw up.

I said, "If you were expecting me to dig into the forty
million, you're nuts. I'd be admitting guilt and leading you
to the loot. No, buddy, your agency has funds earmarked
for these stunts and it will be a pleasure to spend it."

Rice nodded slowly, his eyes spitting animosity. "It will
be forthcoming, Morgan."

"But just to ease your minds," I added, "keep in mind
the premise that I might not *have* that loot."

"For the moment, we're not concerned with that."

"The hell you're not," I laughed. "Now, when does the
action start?"

There was a momentary lull in the conversation, the
hesitation of a man about to go over the top into a place
he might not come back from, then Woolart said,
"Immediately. There will be nothing elaborate about the
procedure at all. You will make all the arrangements for
your own evacuation through sources you will personally
locate. Our cooperation will be in keeping our heads
turned while you accomplish this. For a person of your resources it should prove fairly simple. We will make no attempt to apprehend any of your, er, accomplices, so if you
wish to make use of any friends, feel free to do so."

"You mentioned a crime I was to commit."

"An overt move against the government," Woolart said.
"We'll leave it to your discretion."

"They shoot you for that down there, friend," I reminded him.

"Not when they think you're a person of extreme financial circumstance," he smiled. "They'd much rather extract
your fortune from you."

"And when they do?"

"Then they shoot you," he said.

"Nice people."

"You should be used to them," he said sarcastically. He
picked up a printed sheet and scanned it. "A bank account
containing twenty-five thousand dollars will be opened in

the name of M. A. Winters." He tossed two application cards across the table to me. "Sign those."

I wrote in *M. A. Winters* in the signature space and shoved them back again.

"At the same time," he continued, "in the Miami branch of the same bank we have taken out a safe-deposit box in the same name. You will retain the key. In the box there is a map that supposedly shows the location of your hidden money, but in reality shows one of our places. In the event you are forced to divulge the box and the key we will know you have failed the mission, but if someone else follows that map we at least will have our hands on one of their people who might be able to give us some information."

"Ingenious." I said.

He let my tone of voice pass. "Simple enough to be plausible. There really wouldn't be much else for you to do. A man in your position either has to run or hide. Until now, you've been hiding. Now it's time to run."

"Why?"

There was another of those funny little halts in the sounds that a group of people make. Then Woolart said, "That's simple too. You found a woman."

It came on me like the dawn of a cloudy day, slowly at first, hardly taking shape until it was well established. I looked around at Kimberly Stacy, not quite believing what I had heard. But there wasn't any denying it. That flat, professional, steely look in her eyes gave me the same answer, but I had to be sure. "Her? She's the agent going in with me?"

"That's right, Morgan."

"You people are crazy!"

"We are?"

"How the hell could she contain me?"

Woolart's eyes narrowed into slits. "Miss Stacy has had occasion to shoot five men, Morgan. She's trained in all the skills demanded by her profession and is rated as one of our best operatives. I wouldn't underestimate her."

I was half on my feet, my voice grating in my throat. "Knock it off. You think those people aren't on their toes! You think they couldn't pick off a setup like that? They could spot a tail . . ."

Gavin Woolart shook his head, one corner of his mouth twisted into a wry grin. "I told you we were keeping it simple, Morgan. She won't be tailing you. She's going in as your wife."

My mouth opened to say something, but he cut me off.

"Your legal wife," he said, "in case somebody checks. You're getting married by a J.P. in the State of Georgia."

"*Damn*," I said.

From her side of the room, Kim Stacy said, "It should be an interesting honeymoon, Morgan."

3

THEY LET ME TAKE the shock of it, let it wear off until the sensation was more one of novelty, then briefed me on the people to contact to save me the time of researching the details personally. I had three days before we were to drive south to the Florida Keys where the exodus was to take place and when I insisted on it, they agreed to let me have those three days to myself without having to check in with anyone or having a tail assigned to me. Kim Stacy was going to stay at the Mark Sanford Hotel in case I needed a contact for any reason and would take care of all the final preparations.

When it was over they let me get up and leave just like that.

Crazy, I thought, crazy. All that time on the wanted list; now I walk out on my own and hope I don't get spotted and gunned by some observant cop who doesn't know about the deal. And they trusted me. That was the damned stupid part that choked me. Old Morgan the Raider on the other side of the fence and that little thing inside me wouldn't let me buck the traffic. They did that to old Sir Henry Morgan, too. The Crown gave him a commission and he got rid of their enemies for them. He strung up his old buddies to become a governor . . . but for him the end was different. At least he lived a while to enjoy the fruits of his trickery.

There was only one ironic part to the whole thing. The forty million bucks. They could have nailed me on a dozen different charges but they picked that one to hit me with.

And I didn't have it.

But somebody did and sure as hell they were going to get raided for it.

Mrs. Gustav Timely was affectionately known as Gussie in the trade and had been harboring fugitives at a price for over thirty years. Her operation was neat, but not gaudy, just a mediocre rooming house on the West Side of Manhattan in the middle forties. She kept her mouth shut, asked no questions and had never taken a fall even though a dozen arrests had been made on her premises. In that neighborhood a lot of undesirables had holed up and nobody bothered to stick an elderly widow because a wanted person had checked in under an assumed name.

I rapped on her door and Gussie opened it, her heavy body wrapped in the same cotton bathrobe I had seen her in last. "Morgan," she said.

"Hello, Gussie." I stepped inside without being asked and pushed the door shut.

"You ain't being too smart, Morgan."

"They got you staked out here?"

"Like you wouldn't know." She grunted and made her way to the couch and sat down with a wheeze. "Since you got picked up here I'm marked lousy. I get roused regular and none of the crowd uses the place. I got to depend on them stinking transients or the bunch from the ships."

"You don't seem surprised to see me."

She lit the stub of a butt and blew a cloud of smoke my way. "They all come back sooner or later. Only you ain't staying, Morgan. This time they'd really bounce me."

"No sweat, Gussie."

"So why'd you come?"

"Information."

"I ain't got any."

"Nobody gets hurt and if it pans out you'll make a bundle," I said.

Her massive shoulders heaved in a shrug and she waved one pudgy hand at me. "So ask. It ain't saying I got to answer."

I pulled up a straight-backed chair with my foot and sat down. "Who had my room before me?"

Gussie frowned and said, "Before you got nailed here?"

"Yeah."

"Hell, Morgan . . ." She frowned at me and shrugged again, then reached over into a cracked wicker basket beside the couch and pulled out a ragged ledger. She thumbed back through it until she found what she wanted and nodded thoughtfully. "Character named Melvin Gross. He was a waiter on a ship. Spent his shore time here twice. Kind of a . . ."

"Before that, Gussie."

She poked a couple more pages over with a moistened

forefinger then poked at a name. "Mario Tullius. He came here sick, spent three days in bed, then they took him to Bellevue where he died from pneumonia. Dockhand, I think he was."

"Try another," I told her.

"Gorman Yard. He was here three weeks. Joey Jolley called me to take him on account they had a warrant out on him in Syracuse."

"What for?"

"Hit-and-run. Tagged some pedestrian up there. My money is that he was paid to do it. Looked like that kind. I don't know where he went to after he left." She glanced up at me suspiciously. "What's this all about?"

I didn't answer her. "Try the one before that."

She didn't bother to look it up. "Bernice Case," she said. "Cute little hooker who kept the room three years. No trouble at all. She never brought her marks here with her and slipped me some extra dough whenever she landed a real live one. She did real well, that girl."

"Why'd she stay in a place like this?"

Gussie let out a little grunt that was supposed to be a chuckle. "Sentiment, that's why. Even a prostie can have that, Morgan. She was born here, right up on the top floor. If it wasn't that she found a guy who wanted to marry her she'd be here yet." She squashed the butt out in a wet saucer on the arm of the couch, then let her eyes roll up to meet mine again. "You ain't said what you wanted."

"Guess," I said.

Old Gussie nodded sagely. "You figure one of 'em came back to get something they stashed up there, spotted you and put the squeal in."

"Something like that."

"You're tagging Gorman Yard, ain't you?"

"Maybe."

"He might be the kind if he wanted an in with the cops. A little grease helps out when you got a warrant on you. Want me to check it with Joey Jolley?"

"Never mind. I'll do it myself."

"Go ahead." She grinned through her layers of fat and added, "When you gonna give me a slice of that forty mil, Morgan?"

"Later, baby."

"Well, I know it ain't around here. I like to tore that place apart after the cops got done with it just to make sure you didn't leave it lying around."

"Suppose you found it?"

"Man, would I still be here in this dump?"

Joey Jolley ran a gin mill on the edge of Greenwich Village and dabbled in fencing jewels to keep his hand in. He was an old-time thief who could be counted on to come up with a contact if the price was right.

He met me in his private office that had a side entrance onto the street, a tall lanky guy with a few fronds of hair covering a bald head disguised with a sunlamp tan. "So," he said, "the legendary Morgan. I was beginning to wonder if you ever existed."

"You can't kill a legend, Joey."

"Perhaps not," he smiled. "Now. The point of business. I expect you want to dispose of those forty millions you so carefully kept out of circulation. Unfortunately, they were in serial order, but fortunately of small-enough denomination to pay off, say . . . one for ten?"

"Skip it, Joey. I can get better offers than that."

He stared at me a moment, puzzled, then made a gesture of resignation. "In that case, I'll just raise . . . it is the disposition of the money, isn't it?"

"No."

"Strange. I never heard of you operating through a contact before. I thought you were a loner."

"Where's Gorman Yard?"

For a second his mind ran over the name, then he nodded. "I see. You both lived under Gussie's roof a while, didn't you?"

"That's right."

"Any connection I should know about?"

"Not specially," I said. "He might be able to give me a hand in something."

"Trouble?"

"Nothing that will involve you."

"Can't touch me anyway, Morgan. Yard's doing time at Elmira. They proved a hit-and-run on him a couple of years ago. He's still got another five to do."

"That was a hard fall, Joey."

Jolley shrugged indifferently and said, "Apparently there was some premeditation involved. He had made a deal with the guy that went sour and Yard didn't like it. It's all a matter of public record if you want to look it up."

"Maybe I'll do that. How'd he contact you?"

"I knew him when he was pushing black-market stuff during the war. He had taken a couple of tumbles back then for small stuff before he widened his horizons. He wasn't much good at anything. Whatever he made he always blew on the nags, but he was good for a tab if he ran one up. Not a bad sort at all, if you like rats. Now, may I make a point?"

"Be my guest."

"Since you didn't come here to make a deal on all those lovely bills you raided the Treasury Department for, would you consider me in case you have something planned for the future?"

"My pleasure."

"Can we . . . approximate a time?"

"It won't be long. I'd like to see that cash in circulation too."

"So would I, my boy, so would I. Please be careful. The next time you're caught precautions against your escape will be a little more elaborate. It still surprises me that they didn't take note of your previous escapades. That one in Mexico was a beauty."

I acknowledged the compliment with a wink, got up and went out through the side door. I flagged a cruising cab, went back to the old neighborhood and started making the rounds.

New York is a peculiar place. Although it's divided into five boroughs it's really a complex of thousands of components, each enjoying a strange autonomy. There are no visible divisions except the street signs, but the boundaries are there, the perimeters guarded and respected, the rules observed. Outsiders are ignored like the shadows, but those within are subject to the regulations.

I was neither. Oh, they knew me there all right. I was less than a shadow and bigger than the rules. Their eyes were sharp and word travels fast. I could ask and be answered, but not asked about. My kind of trouble was beyond their realm of comprehension and they wanted no part of Morgan the Raider. But at least I could ask questions and get the answers if they had them to give.

Baldy Hines, who ran the delicatessen, remembered Gorman Yard because he had a habit of dropping a fifty-dollar bill on the counter for a pack of cigarettes. Baldy never checked the serial numbers out, but they had been new bills, good enough for him and bankable. Several times he had seen Yard with a couple of guys from across town who dressed like they had a bundle, but he couldn't identify them. Once Bernice Case came back to see some old friends and he had tried to put the make on her, but she had slammed him one in the puss and Yard dropped that bit of action. Miss Case didn't like to clutter up her own doorsteps no matter what she did for a living.

Across the street Ma Toppett who spent half her life hanging out the front window leaning on a chair cushion, watching the neighbors for diversion, had a little more to add. She poured me coffee while her husband snored away in front of a blaring television set and told me about Yard making some quiet exits from the house into a black Caddie on several different occasions. The car simply stopped, he got in, so it had probably been prearranged. She didn't spot the driver or the plate number and didn't care one way or another except that it gave her something to speculate about. She remembered Mario Tullius too and had brought him some hot soup once before they took him away. While he was eating she had a chance to look around, but all she saw was a gold watch, a few books and some small bills sticking out of his wallet on his dresser. She added the bit that it was Bernice Case who paid his remaining rent to old Gussie after he died, but that wasn't unusual because the little hooker was always doing something nice for the people in her old neighborhood.

I didn't like to ask, but there were still two more leads to take. It was a quarter to twelve and outside things were coming to a slow halt. The late night sounds had started . . . sirens wailing on the humid air as the prowl cars answered their calls, an occasional muffled giggle from a darkened hallway, the raucous yell of a few kids who had no enforced bedtime, and the blare of TV news announcers giving the latest in the world's troubles.

On the corner I grabbed a cab and had him take me to the Mark Sanford Hotel, registered as M. A. Winters and called Kim Stacy to see if she was in.

There was no sleep in her voice, just that cool, efficient, curious tone and she told me to come on up.

A long time ago the world had become a small place to me and the things that happen in it were common place. I thought there could be no more suprises and never a shocker because I had seen it all and had been through the grinder too many times not to know what was on the other end.

But I was wrong.

She opened the door to my knock and stood there surveying me a long second, the backlighting oozing through the sheer nylon housecoat, the smell of her a fragrant temptation that was like little hands reaching out to feel you, their wild fingertips touching all the sensitive spots, until satisfied, they withdrew and beckoned an invitation to come closer.

I forced a grin past the tight feeling on my face and said, "Hi, doll. Talk time?"

Her eyebrows raised quizzically and a suggestion of a smile played around her mouth. "Come in, Morgan."

She stepped aside and I went past her, my arm making the minutest accidental contact with the tips of her breasts, but that slight touch was charged with a delicate emotional jolt and those feathery fingers hit me right in the pit of the stomach again.

Kim Stacy wasn't the person I had seen the first time. The ingrained attitude of the professional huntress was gone, hidden somewhere under the natural veneer of the female. There was only that cool softness of *girl* flavored with the desire to be transformed into the warm hardness of woman that was here now. The wide violet eyes were filled with casual humor and through lips that blossomed in a small, lush smile she said, "Morgan . . . just because we're somewhat engaged . . ."

Then I laughed and everything was all right and I felt the heat leave me. A second ago I had damn near been lost for the first time since I made the initial mistake and had gotten shot for it. Now things were real again and in their right place.

"Drink?" she asked me.

"Got a cold beer?"

She nodded, went into the kitchen alcove and came back with a frosted can of Pabst. "Glass?"

"Can's fine. Join me?"

She stretched her smile a little further. "I don't think so. You mentioned talk. Are you ready to move out?"

I perched on the arm of the big chair and sipped the top off the beer. "Not quite. First I want you people to do something for me."

Something happened to the smile. An air of professionalism clouded the expression of her face and she was examining me again, alert to every word, every nuance. "You aren't in a position to be asking favors, Morgan. You were told that."

"But I am, baby. You've been told that too."

Her eyes narrowed slightly, then she shrugged and said,

"Very well, I can pass it along anyway." She watched me, waiting.

I said, "There's a guy in Elmira named Gorman Yard. I want all the information on him I can get. Oh, I could do it myself, but you can do it quicker."

"Is that all?"

"No. I want something else that never came out at my trial."

"Oh?"

"Outside the loot they found stashed in my room, how much of that forty million was ever recovered from public circulation. Think you can manage that?"

"Perhaps. Would you mind telling me why you want this information?"

"Sure. I want to see where I went wrong." I gave her a big grin and she knew I was lying, but she nodded anyway.

"Suppose they won't supply the answers," Kim asked me.

"Funny things might happen, sugar," I told her. "Like a nosy newspaperman I knew. He'd love a slice of this action to sell a few more papers."

"They wouldn't let it happen, Morgan."

"You don't know my friends, Kid." I finished the beer and set the empty on the back of the chair. "Tomorrow?"

"I'll try."

I got up, walked to the door, then turned and looked at her a few seconds. "Do you have any special instructions on this assignment, Kim?"

Those slanted eyes gave me a curious glance. "What do you mean?"

"Our impending marriage. Is it to be consummated?"

A slow flush burned its way past her shoulders and throat into her face. "When I have a man," she said slowly, "I'll do the choosing."

"Smart," I said. "The agency is really thinking. Non-consummation of a marriage is grounds for a divorce action. You get off the hook very nicely, don't you?"

"Yes, really I do."

"Only they forgot something." My grin got bitter.

This time her voice was unexpectedly small. "What?"

"There's no law against a man raping his own wife," I said as I went out the door.

I had conformed to the ground rules they had laid down

for me by registering at the hotel, but for three days the course of action was my own. If I needed security I wanted to make it myself. Before I had gone into the deal a few loners and a nicely organized bunch had tried to tap me out for the big bundle they thought I had cached somewhere and it took plenty of slipping and sliding with a bullet crease along my hip and some broken heads on the other side before I set up a cover they couldn't penetrate. I didn't want it to start again. This way was bad enough.

The hotel I picked was a commercial-residential type on Sixth Avenue where your business was your own and the surroundings common enough to lose yourself in. I paid in advance, got on the phone and by two-thirty I had located Bernice Case and got back into the night world where I belonged.

André's was a far-out kind of bar that serviced the office crowd during the day, the weirdos until midnight and the odd breed until he closed. His specialty was chili if you had the stomach for the firepower he could lay in it and being a two-bowl man myself, he always had an appreciative grin for my patronage.

She was sitting in the last booth dipping her chili out with Ritz crackers, absorbed in the early edition of *The News,* and when I sat down opposite her she gave me a strange little glance and said, "Hungry?"

In a funny way, she was like a friendly kitten. She had siezed me up, figured me to be broke, and knowing she was always good for a touch, was ready to share her plate.

I had seen a lot of hookers in my time. There were prostitutes in the trade because they didn't know any better, some because they were forced into it and others because they liked it. But the mark of it was always there. It showed in their eyes that reflected the tired worldliness of a sordid life or in the expression that was disgust at themselves or the ones who used them, and sometimes in the early age lines that stamped years instead of days on their faces and bodies. The strange thing about Bernice Case was the curious lack of any of these things. If there was anything there it was compassion. Her eyes had a happy smile in them and her mouth was a red bloom of pleasure. Her blond hair had a silk-shine to it and was a dark enough blond to be real. She still had a young-girl freshness in the tilt of her breasts and the naturally indolent way she made her body move.

"No. But thanks anyway, Bernice," I said.

Her head tilted at the mention of her name. "Do I know you?"

"Not personally. We have some mutual friends." I grinned at her and folded the paper shut.

Even white teeth bit into her lower lip and she let out a small chuckle and wrinkled her nose at me. "I wish my friends would observe my working schedule." She reached out and touched my hand. "Look, I'm not trying to hurt your feelings or anything, but it's been a long evening and . . ."

I shook my head. "You and me both, Bernice. Let's say I don't want to see you, ah, professionally."

"That's a nice way to put it," she laughed.

"And I don't need a handout," I added.

"At least you're different." She scratched one manicured fingernail along the back of my wrist and took her hand away. "These mutual friends . . ." she began.

"Old Gussie, Ma Toppett."

Her eyes squinted slightly, then she leaned back and looked at me with interest. "You're not from the neighborhood," she stated.

"Since your time. I boarded with Old Gussie until the fuzz nailed me."

The recognition came into her face slowly and she pursed her mouth and nodded sagely. "You're Morgan, aren't you?"

"That's right."

"You're crazy coming around here, you know. I didn't spot you right off, but some of these characters will turn in their own mothers for drinking money. Maybe I don't have a memory for faces that looked at me from the front page, but they have."

"I'll worry about that."

Bernice gave me a gesture of mock astonishment and learned her chin on her hands. "Swell, big friend, but what about me? In come the bluecoats, you get nailed and I get tagged as an accomplice. I have a reputation to protect."

"So we'll go somewhere else."

"Like my place, maybe?"

"Suits me."

Once again she studied my face, drawing on all the things she had learned from life and experience, then said quietly, "This is serious, isn't it?"

"Very serious, kid."

"And I can help?"

"Maybe."

"Then let's go to my place."

The building was old, but remodeled, and her apartment was a three-room affair furnished with taste and simplicity. She had indulged herself in an oversized stereo set with a rack of at least a hundred classical records and three paintings by well-known contemporary artists. While she built us a drink she saw me staring at the pictures, and said, "I didn't buy them." She grinned and added, "It wasn't an even trade, either."

"They're worth a bundle, you know."

"Now they are. At the time they were starving artists who needed rent and refrigerator money and I liked their work enough to grubstake them."

I tapped the smallest of the three frames. "This guy's last effort just went for over a hundred G's."

"Uh-huh." She handed me a rye and ginger in a tall glass.

"Why don't you sell them?"

Very simply, she said, "I like them." She walked to the record player, pushed a button, then sat down and crossed one lovely leg over the other. "You had something to ask me, Morgan."

I took the chair opposite the strange little blonde and sipped at my drink. "How much do you know about me?"

"As much as the papers said." Her eyes twinkled over the glass at me. "I know they didn't get the rest of that money you . . . appropriated."

"Why don't you say 'stole'?"

"Because it was government money. Hell's bells, they take enough away in taxes and blow it on a bunch of nitheads in places you never heard of to make it easier for people to hate us, so I'm damn glad to see them get nicked for a change. Boy, I bet they were mad."

"They were furious."

"You going to give it back?"

"Should I?"

Bernice giggled like a childish conspirator and made a screwy face. "Not yet. If it's too hot to spend, make them hurt a little bit, then maybe send it back in an old beer carton or something. Can you imagine their faces? Maybe they'll think it's a bomb and dunk it in oil like they do and ruin the whole batch themselves."

I took a long pull at the drink. "You're crazy."

"It's a crazy world. At least you can have fun."

"Are you?"

For a moment her eyes took on a soft expression. "Let's say I like people."

"Then you're better than I am, kid. I can't be that generous."

A little twitch of sympathy touched her mouth. "We were talking about something, Morgan."

I eased back in the chair and spun the glass around in my hand. "You knew Gorman Yard, didn't you?"

"Yes."

"Any opinions?"

Her face took on a straightforward expression then. "Since you don't want facts, you must know about him."

I nodded.

"He was a pig," she said. "I don't like pigs."

"How?"

"If he had a choice to be nice or nasty, he'd be rotten."

"This from personal experience?"

"He couldn't have enough money to buy me, Morgan. He tried, though. I told him once that I had a couple of friends . . . real friends . . . I could talk to them and he'd never be able to say anything again. He knew I wasn't fooling."

"What did he pull?"

Her eyes widened blandly and she said, "Morgan, unless you've seen real filth, you can't imagine what kind of a person Gorman Yard could be. Oh, it wasn't only him. He had to associate with his own kind. They can only stand each other anyway . . . no one else will have anything to do with them. I saw him with people I knew about. Some I didn't know, but they had to be like him. I was surprised Old Gussie even let him in her place, but lately, she isn't as particular as she was. If she ever knew about that creep he used to shack up with she'd flip."

"What creep?"

"Ever see a lizard stare at you, Morgan?"

I shrugged.

"Garfish do it too. They rise to the top like a small submarine and stare at you with those damn horrible eyes and if you haven't got a gun to shoot them with they just go back down again and it's like you had been eaten alive with those eyes." She took a quick swallow of her drink and balanced the glass on the palm of one hand. "When I was a kid my uncle used to take me fishing. I remember the gars."

"Who was this guy, Bernice?"

"Beats me. He didn't poke his head out very often. He

was there for a while, then he was gone. I saw him across
the airshaft from Lily Temple's room a couple of times.
She was afraid of him too." She paused, thinking, then
said, "He gave you that itchy feeling that he was hooked
on H. You know, that trapped-rat sort of thing? Only he
wasn't. I've seen too many of them. He didn't take any
trips into never-never land. It looked like he was already
there."

"Maybe they were in business together," I suggested.

"Not Gorman Yard. He was a loner. I'd say this guy
was on the run and Yard was taking advantage of it."

"Yard was on the run too."

"Not like this one was. What gets me is that his kind
doesn't get scared easily. I wouldn't want to mess with
him. If he and Yard were working a deal, I didn't get it.
Anyway, he wasn't there long. Maybe a couple of weeks
at the most."

"How do you know?"

"Because I know what Yard bought at the deli. I know
when he quit bringing in all those goodies. He was buying
for two; then all of a sudden he quit and it was pretty
soon after that the cops picked him up and slapped him in
the cooler."

"You mentioned some others," I said.

"More creeps," she told me. "That guy was plain looking for trouble. You know, he starts hanging out with
some of the shooters Whitey Tass keeps around, angling
for an introduction to the big man himself, and he's damn
lucky he got picked up by the fuzz before Whitey got
sore. He runs too big an operation in the city to be bugged
by a pig like Yard. One day Lou Steubal tried to get an
inside track with Whitey, levering him on account of what
Whitey did to his sister, and they found Lou in the drink.
It looked like Lou got gassed up and fell in, but don't try
to tell me that. Whitey had him tapped out."

"Nice people."

"And now you're asking around. Could I ask why?"

"Sure, you could."

"But you're not about to tell me."

"That's right."

"Why?"

"Like the man said, Bernice, a little bit of information
can be a bad thing."

She gave me that twisted little grin again and nodded.
"You're right, of course. I don't really want to know except out of curiosity. But can I guess?"

"If you like."

Bernice studied her glass, drained half of it and set it on the floor beside the chair. "You lived in the house and Gorman Yard lived there too. He was there first, so I'll suppose that he left something there, came back to get it and spotted you. Maybe he turned on the heat and got you nailed.

I shook my head and finished my drink.

"Then I'll suppose this," she said. "When those Treasury Agents shook Gussie's place down and found that sailor with a load of H on him, then uncovered your little nest egg in a general search and grabbed you, it was because Yard knew you were there, but blew the whistle on the sailor, hoping to get you running so he could pick up the loot you had hidden."

"That's a good suppose if it were true," I told her.

Her impish eyes twinkled at me. "I was born in that house, Morgan. That place you hid all that cash wasn't new to me. I used to keep things there when I was a kid. My old man built it to hide the booze from my mother. How did you find it?"

I shrugged and said nothing.

"Well, there weren't too many places to hide anything in that fleabag. You didn't have much choice. What gets me is where the rest of it is. Gussie ripped up everything but the foundations looking for it after they got you."

"Maybe you have an idea."

"Sure," she grinned. "You're not one to keep all your eggs in one basket. The rest of it never was there or I would have found it. I went back and poked around in all my old hiding places too."

"I hate to have been such a disappointment, kid."

"You weren't. It was fun." She paused, then said, "It's been an odd conversation, Morgan. Did I say anything important?"

"Possibly," I told her. "How badly did you want that money?"

"Really, not at all. I do all right."

"Care to earn a few bucks?"

"How?"

"Think you can find out why Gorman Yard wanted to get close to Whitey Tass?"

"That's a maybe, Morgan. Those people don't like to talk much, even to one of their own. I can give it a try, though. I've had . . . dealings with one the last six months." Then her eyes met mine and locked seriously.

"But not for money, Morgan. I'll do it, but not for money."

"I don't like being obligated, baby."

"Can you like me a little? I've never really been liked before."

"You've been loved at one time, sugar."

"Not love, Morgan. I just want to be liked. I want one real friend who isn't afraid."

"I'm scared all the time," I said.

"But not afraid. That's why you're on the outside no matter what they tried to do to you."

I felt the smile tug at my mouth and threw her a wink. "I like you, kitten. That I really do."

"Then you know I'm going to keep you here tonight. I don't want any of the things I . . . have to do with other people. I just want to be held and liked and to talk about little things, listen to some music, hold hands and maybe fall asleep on your shoulder until the sun comes up. Do you know what I mean, Morgan."

I got up and walked over to her and ran my fingers through the silken clouds of her hair and looked into the funny, friendly eyes and nodded.

"I know," I said.

4

I GOT OUT of the cab in front of my hotel and stared at the nearly empty streets of the city that hadn't struggled back to life yet. A wet mist slicked the streets, and the tops of the buildings were smothered by low-hanging clouds.

When I reached my room I slept until two in the afternoon, then got on the phone to Miami and laid out my program with Art Keefer to get me and Kim out of the country. He thought I was nuts picking the place I wanted to go when a few better ones were another day's flight further south where a guy could hide out all his life if he wasn't an Eichmann and had the money to grease a few palms. But I insisted and he went along with me like he always did and told me when and where we'd meet. The second call got me Little Joe Malone, who promised to deliver a few necessary items to a locker in the bus station with the key left downstairs at the desk for me.

At four thirty I picked up the key, paid my bill and hopped a cab uptown, picked up the .45 and box of ammo, a set of picks and two small files that had the biting edge of an acetelene torch. A half hour later I was knocking on Kim Stacy's door and heard her cross the room to open it for me.

"Hello, my betrothed," I said.

"Let's not make too much of a game of it, Morgan."

"Everything's a game, Kim. It's only the stakes that change."

She shut the door behind me and followed me inside, waited until I had settled myself in the big chair, then sat crosswise on the one by the desk. "You weren't here last night."

"Did it matter?"

"My people didn't like it."

"Screw your people."

"Your part of this operation is voluntary."

"Okay, so I'm back."

Kim nodded, but there was a shadow of accusation in her eyes. "Not that it will matter to you," she told me, "but I have signed a receipt for your person and until I in turn sign you over to your next custodian, my neck and career are on the block. I didn't ask for this duty. I didn't want it. But it was offered to me and I accepted it. Since your acceptance was of a voluntary nature I was hoping our arrangement would be to our mutual satisfaction. There's no reason for either of us getting hurt."

"Oh, honey," I said, "come off it. Hell, if I wanted to exercise my talents I'd take on the whole damn department you represent, not pick on just you. Now knock it off, okay?"

Reluctantly, and with a dour grin, she said, "Okay, Morgan. We'll stay loose and cool."

"Sure. Now . . . anything on Gorman Yard?"

For a few seconds she worried her lip with her teeth. "He's dead, Morgan."

"What!"

"There was an industrial accident in the prison machine shop. No one was held responsible." She stopped, watched my reaction, then folded her arms on the back of the chair. "Since you were the one to institute the inquiry, they've started another investigation."

"That should be fun with those boys up there. They won't get very far. How did the cops nail him in the first place?"

"They ware tipped off to his whereabouts by an anonymous phone call. They followed up the story the informer gave them and made the charge stick. It was all cut and dry. Yard even confessed and didn't try very hard to fight his conviction. It was almost as if he preferred being sent up."

"That might just be the way it was."

"Oh?"

"Nothing. What about the rest of my forty million?"

"So far, nothing has appeared. All possible outlets for bills of that denomination with those serial numbers had been alerted. You did a good job of it. The only trouble is, the heat's not going to go off in this case. You can pass that on to the rest of your friends you worked that robbery out with."

"I'm a loner, Kim. You saw my record."

"This time you weren't. It took more than one person to engineer that job. You pulled the same stunt twice during the war, getting those troop-movement plans and coordinates on the German blockhouses from their armored cars. You even laid it out ahead of time in Allied Headquarters, the booby-trap devices to stop their vehicles at a given spot, the D-Y gas to knock out the occupants without them ever knowing what had happened and the means of entry with that compact torch unit they devised for you. Only this time you improved your technique. There was no torch. It was more like an acid burn. They still can't figure it. What did you use, Morgan?"

Somehow her tone had changed to one of mild respect and I grinned at her. "We had six men on that deal, honey."

"I know. We looked into that too, wondering if they decided to beome accomplices in a bigger haul. Three are dead; one was a rather severe casualty and later disappeared into the limbo of Australia and the German national you worked with is now a staid, successful businessman in Berlin. No, you're the only one left, the only one who could plan and execute a coup like that one."

"I accept your applause."

"It's too bad you're not worth it."

"Nuts."

"At least this way you can redeem yourself a little bit."

"Nuts to that, too," I said.

"Your funeral, Morgan."

"Maybe." I looked at my watch. It was almost six thirty. "You packed?" I asked her.

Puzzle lines touched her forehead. "Why?"

"Because we're leaving on our honeymoon."

She seemed to stiffen and her mouth went tight. "You said . . . you wanted three days."

"Then let's just say I can't wait any longer. If I have to do this on my own I'm going to do it my own way. Get your bags packed. I have a car waiting downstairs. You're on orders, so don't buck me. Like you said, stay loose and cool. The worst of it is still ahead."

We were married in Georgia near the Florida line at a little place that specialized in "Marriage Certificate, Blood Test and Ceremony, One Hour." My lack of any name but Morgan almost stopped the JP until I came up with my Army discharge papers and suggested their style of NFN-NMI, no first name-no middle initial; then he was ready for his routine.

It wasn't the happiest of weddings because Kim looked

too nervous and I as too damn tired to react like a normal bridegroom should. When I kissed her as custom required and the JP and witnesses expected, it was more like a couple of fighters touching gloves before the first round began. But maybe it wasn't such an abnormal reaction at that. The fee and tip were collected with a toothy smile and a hearty "good luck" while our first witness went to the phone to get the notice into the local paper.

When we got back to the car Kim sat a little farther over than she had been and without looking at me said, "Now what?"

"We make it look real, pet. We cross the state line, register at a motel and get some sleep."

I knew what she was thinking, but she didn't say it. Her nod was one of perfunctory agreement, but a little shudder seemed to run across her shoulders and took the edge off for me. It's always good to have a broad a little scared of you. I grinned at my reflection in the windshield, turned on the ignition and got back out on the highway.

At dusk I spotted the Flora Palm Ranch Motel and turned in the pebbled driveway. Being off season, there were only a few other cars, but two of them had "Just Married" slogans painted on their sides and were festooned with ribbons and shredded pieces of crepe paper. I said, "We're in good company, Kim."

"Please."

"Don't worry; I'll get twin beds."

The clerk handed me the register and took my money without a second glance and slid a key to Number 20 across the counter. I left a wake-up call for six, then pulled the car down to our room and unloaded the two bags and stuck them inside the room. I had to have at least one kick out of the deal, so as Kim walked by I scooped her up in my arms and carried her inside. She let out a sudden, sharp gasp and froze momentarily in my arms until I put her down.

"It's an old custom, sugar. I've never been married before."

Very slowly the frost left her face and she smiled gently at me. One hand touched my cheek and she raised herself on her toes and touched her mouth against mine. It was only for a second, but the rich softness of her lips was bedded in warmth their moistness couldn't quench.

"I'm sorry, Morgan. It was sweet of you. I've never been married before either. Thank you."

"The government has some screwy regulations. I hope you know all the rules."

"I do. I hope you observe them."

"Don't trust me too far, doll," I grinned at her. "And don't depend on your karate training."

"Now we're back to that again," she laughed. "How about this?"

In her hand she held a tiny black automatic and the snout was pointed right at my belly. But she didn't see my hand move and suddenly the big hole in the end of the .45 in my fist was staring at a spot between her eyes. "How about that?" I asked her.

"What a wonderful way to begin a marriage. I get your message, Morgan; now can we get to business?"

"My pleasure, sweetheart."

For twenty minutes she was on the phone to her people, her guarded conversation giving the details of the wedding and our location. Evidently she was told to go ahead on her own; then for a full five minutes she did nothing but listen. When she hung up she swung around with an impatient gesture and said, "We're to proceed as planned. There's only one change."

I felt the hairs on the back of my neck bristle. "What change?"

"The agency feels that we'll have to move faster. They're sending in word of our arrival."

"Those stupid. . ."

She waved a hand to shut me up. "Not through our people. It will come from their own sources. More a rumor than anything else. At least we'll be expected and you won't have to do all the groundwork."

"That's the key to the success of this thing. Don't they know that?"

"I'm sure they know what they're doing."

"Damn it, they'd better."

"Do you mind tell me what arrangements you've made?"

"When the time comes," I told her.

I picked up the telephone and gave a New York number to the switchboard. After the third ring it was picked up and a voice said, "Joey Jolley here."

"Morgan, Joey."

"Ah, you've reconsidered—"

I cut him off. "No dice yet, Joey. Let things jell first."

"If that's the way it has to be. What can I do for you?"

"Gorman Yard is dead."

"Yes, I know," he told me without any emotion. "I took

the trouble to make inquiries. My source tells me the accident he sustained wasn't of his own doing. Naturally, nobody's talking, but you know the grapevine. Somebody inside there got orders to cool Mr. Yard and did an excellent job of it."

"That's what I was afraid of," I said.

"Incidentally, he isn't the only one from that neighborhood who took the big trip.

Something tightened in the pit of my stomach. "Go on."

"I just heard the TV report that the body of a girl found strangled to death an hour ago has been identified as Bernice Case. They suggested she was a lady of the evening and probably was killed in the pursuit of her occupation. Or is that simply a cover job, Morgan?"

My hand felt as though it would break the receiver into bits. Damn, they had gotten to her. One lovely, lonely girl who only wanted to be liked. One poor little hooker who gave more than she took. They had to go and slam her. I kept my voice as normal as possible and said, "I can't see the connection, Joey. You know the racket she was in."

He let a few seconds pass. "Possibly. The mob doesn't appreciate individual operators. If they hit her because she didn't pay off they could be in real trouble. I understand she was a well-liked kid."

But she didn't know that, I thought.

"Any action on it?"

"Rough talk around the neighborhood. Somebody's going to get their ass wiped with a cob if they find out who was behind it. Old Gussie is leading the parade and you know her."

"Tough. Wish I could do something."

"Sure there's no connection?"

"Not on my end," I lied. "What I wanted to know was the inside on Whitey Tass."

"You kidding?" Joey said. His voice said I should know better than to ask. "If it's big it's got his name on it, but he still commands a political power in his section that keeps the heat off better than fiberglass. He's growing, Morgan. Keep clear of him."

"I intend to. That's why I'm calling you. See what you can get."

"Facts or rumors?"

"Either one. Both are probably true."

"One's easier to get." He coughed, then added, "The things I'll do for a slice of that forty mil amaze me, Morgan."

"Just remember that it's all on speculation."

"I'll trust your reputation. How do I reach you?"

"You can't, I said. "I'll call you."

I hung up and turned around. The muscles in my back and shoulders were bunched into knots and I could feel the tightness drawing my mouth into a flat line. Kim watched me a moment, saying nothing, knowing I had to get it out of me anyway.

When I felt like bursting I said softly, "Bernice Case. She was my friend. They killed her for nothing."

I didn't have to say anything more. She'd remember the name and call it in and all those big agencies could go to work on it and if they were smart they'd put things together and work it out with the ones in the neighborhood who could be just as efficient in their own way. And if they didn't do it, I'd be back and do it for them.

A promise, Bernice, for that wonderful night of just lying there on the sofa with you in my arms, warm and soapy smelling from a hot shower, with the perfume in your hair and that crazy Hawaiian mu-mu that seemed to glow in the darkness and all that silly talk about when we were kids. You were well liked, little kitty cat.

I flopped on the bed and closed my eyes. In a few minutes I heard the bedsprings next to me creak. Outside, the tree frogs peeped an endless tune and far off I could hear the traffic on the highway going by.

Kim's voice was very quiet when she asked, "Was she your girl, Morgan?"

"I only saw her once," I said.

For the second time that night she said, "I'm sorry." For that one moment she was a woman, and not a trained pro playing watchdog to a fugitive.

By sunup we were on the road, picked up the Florida Turnpike and headed toward Miami. Traffic was light, but every twenty miles we'd have to bust our way through a thunderstorm and with the windows up the car was like the inside of a Bessemer Converter. I made a quick stop at the bank where Gavin Woolart had established an account for me, got a checkbook and with the first one drew out twenty thousand in handy denomination bills and folded them into my pocket. No one seemed concerned about the transaction, though there were several curious glances thrown my way. I figured Woolart had set up the deal so that I'd look like one of his own people and no questions

were to be asked. Kim was mopping her face when I got
back in the car and it felt like it was still getting hotter. I
picked up the Palmetto Highway, swept around the Miami
area and headed down into the Keys. Both of us were
soaked in our own sweat by the time we reached the
Grove Motel.

While Kim headed for the shower, I went down the
road, brought a six-pack of Pabst and put in a call for Art
Keefer from a pay station. He said he'd be by in an hour,
so I went back to the motel, parked in the slot beside our
room and went inside.

Kim wasn't there, but her clothes were hung up near
the air conditioner and her suitcase was open on the bed.
From the back I could hear a couple of kids yelling
around the pool, looked out and saw the back of her head
in one of the lounge chairs, then showered, climbed into
my trunks and went out with a can of beer in each hand.

And almost dropped them.

In a black-and-white bikini that would have been invisible had it not contrasted so sharply with the gold of her
skin, she was stretched out languidly, her lovely body lying
in a provocative S curve. It was a dizzy, instant experience
to see the heady swell of her breasts that dipped into the
hollow of her stomach, then flowed into the rise of her
hips and melted into the warm, sweeping fullness of her
thighs and calves.

I sat on the end of the lounge quickly and handed her a
can. "Have a cold one."

A smile danced around her mouth as she took it. "I
didn't think you could be affected like that."

"When I marry I sure can pick them," I said. "Sorry, but
you surprised me." I tasted the beer, licked my lips and let
my eyes roam over her again. "You have a hell of a
shape, baby."

"So I've been told. At times it's useful to disconcert
somebody."

"I'm disconcerted. You did a magnificent job."

The little smile drifted away then. "Don't take it to
heart. It's only a temporary arrangement."

I couldn't let her get away with it. I let my mouth twist
in a nasty grin and said, "Only if I want it that way.
Don't forget it."

The way her stomach sucked in a fraction said she got
the message but she pretended to ignore it with, "Did you
make your contact?"

I nodded.

"Can you tell me now?"

I finished the can of beer and tossed the empty in a wire basket behind me. "Tomorrow we charter a fishing boat that leaves from a private docking area. At noon we'll be out about twelve miles; Art Keefer will pick up up in a seaplane, fly us offshore a mile from our destination where we'll be met by another boat and taken in. After that we'll play it by ear."

"Is this . . . the usual arrangement?"

"The pattern varies," I said. I let out a small laugh. "After all, people like us don't like being nailed by the cops. It's a way of life."

"A stupid way."

"Maybe for you, kid. It's hard to explain. I'm assuming you're smart enough not to try to bust any of these people. Not that you can. They're clever enough to keep themselves covered."

"My orders read that way," she said. "We're not interested in the little people."

"Kid, you got a lot to learn," I told her. "My friend is doing us a favor. Taking us in will be easy. He's putting his neck on the line getting us out."

"No he isn't."

I turned slowly and looked at her. She focused her eyes on my face and said, "The return trip will be under our direction. You see, we're not taking any chances on losing you along the line."

"You're crazy, sugar. What makes you think I won't cut out anytime?"

"Because you're made like that. Now you're having fun."

"I've changed my mind before."

"That's why I'm wearing the bikini," she said. "At least it will keep you thinking of other things. Not that it will do you any good," she added.

My grin got nice and tight this time. "Why does the female have the unholy idea she can conquer the male?"

"Can't she?" There was the slightest haughty tone to her voice.

"Only some," I said. "Only some, baby."

Then Art Keefer came up and rescued us both from the conversation. He was a big, rangy guy with corded forearms and hair bleached almost white from the sun, skin like tanned leather and bright green eyes that had looked on the world and thrown it away. He had the indelible stamp of the adventurer, a perpetual cynical twist to his mouth, scars from a dozen battles etched into the lines of his face.

His reaction to Kim was almost the same as mine, the sudden appreciation but tempered with regret because right now she belonged to me. I hadn't seen him for seven years, but nobody would have known it. He threw me a wink and said, "Hello, jailbird."

"They didn't keep me long enough to rate the compliment, Art."

"Somebody should have clued them in. How'd you do it?"

"Rubber bars," I laughed "Meet Kim Stacy . . . or rather, Mrs. Morgan."

"My pleasure," he said.

Kim held out her hand and he took it, but the introduction was one of two animals sizing each other up. When he stepped back he looked at me quickly and I got his meaning. I said, "It's a clean deal, Art. No repercussions."

"You're nuts, buddy. There are other ways."

"I like it this way."

"Sure, you always did. But then, you always were nuts too."

"Everything ready?"

Art said softly. "Six A.M. at Raymond's. Travel light. I want as much fuel aboard as I can carry. How much does she know?"

"The works."

"There's something else. You're expected. Vince got the word an hour ago and sent it out on shortwave. Who planted it?"

Kim said matter-of factly, "We did."

Art looked at me, his eyes curious now. "That okay with you?"

"They had to expedite matters."

"You're going to have plenty of company, then. Right now their regime is damn rocky and with that loot they think they can extract from you they can get back on their feet. They're going to want to expedite matters too. I wouldn't want to be in your shoes."

I glanced at Kim and laughed. "The hell you wouldn't."

Art grinned and shrugged. "I don't know how you always get the best end of the deal."

"Pure good luck," I said. "All the other details standard or have things changed?"

"Four points up on the old wavelength and use the same Kissler code. They still haven't broken that one.

Somebody will be monitoring around the clock and if you need a contact, try the one at the Orino Bar who'll sing our old song as a recognition gimmick."

"Any heavies in the act?"

"Watch out for one called Russo Sabin. He's a hatchet man for Carlos Ortega who's about to take the power away from the present government. He has civilian and military personnel behind him and we know damn well he's been buttering up to the Commies, who will jump right in and back him if he wins this political battle. All Ortega needs is a few million to grease the right palms and we're going to have another Cuba on our hands."

"How does it look?"

"Right now, all in his favor. You're going to be a welcome addition to his program." Art paused and looked at the both of us a second. "Any interagency cooperation here?"

"Why?"

"The Navy and the Border Patrol are pretty damn tight, old buddy."

"Good. It has to look right. They haven't been alerted, so it's all your operation."

"As long as I know."

"If we get hit it will be our own fault. Nobody gets off the hook."

"They haven't caught me yet," Art said. We shook hands; he nodded to Kim and stalked away with a fierce stride, disappearing around the corner of the building.

Kim watched him go, then said, "He seems very proficient."

"He has to be," I told her.

Something made her look at me sharply. "Who is he?"

"One of the men you said was dead. We were part of that team that operated behind the lines in Germany during the war."

"But . . . there was no Keefer . . ." she started.

I laughed and shook my head. "He was in the Army under a different name then."

Her eyes looked almost black under the frown. "Then the other three . . ."

"Oh, *two* of them are dead, all right."

She kept studying me and I knew what she was thinking. I shook my head slowly and said. "He wasn't any part of that forty-million-dollar haul, sugar. Forget it."

Overhead there was the dull rumble of thunder and the sun slid behind an ominous bank of black clouds. The two kids in the pool came out of the water and scurried into their room. I took the empty can from Kim's hand, tossed it into the basket and waved my thumb at our door. "Go get dressed. I'll give you five minutes."

She uncurled from the lounge, stood up and stretched deliberately, legs spread apart, back arched so that I could see every glorious inch of her undulating in the posture. Then she relaxed and looked at me with a chuckle. "You'd better wait ten," she said. "There may be people watching. You wouldn't want them to see you like that, would you?"

5

WE LET DOWN offshore, circling into the stream of the flare Art had dropped. Less than a mile away the stark white crescent of a beach sparkled in the blazing sunlight, like a shark's mouth against the somber green of the hills beyond it. Beneath us a small boat waited, its exhaust puffing little ringlets of smoke.

The touchdown was gentle and Art taxied up to the boat, waiting, facing the wind while the swarthy little guy at the wheel pulled up alongside us. I handed out the bag Kim and I shared, then helped her onto the strut and watched while she leaped to the deck as graceful as a cat. Then Art gave me a few final words of caution and advice before I followed her.

Kim had said little during the flight, preferring to study our backs from a seat behind us. Our easy familiarity had made an impression on her. It was evident our association was of long standing and that without hesitation we had fallen into habit patterns formed by long training and longer experience. It was a situation she didn't like and if I hadn't taken the precaution of jimmying the phone the night before and locking us both in the room she would have phoned in a report of the unusual occurrence. At least it had made her mad enough so she tumbled into bed with her clothes on, ignoring me in the big chair by the door. Once near dawn I heard the metallic *snick* of the safety going off on her automatic, so I deliberately thumbed back the hammer of the .45 with an audible click that told the whole story once and for all and she never moved the rest of the night.

Now she watched me wave Art off, her face impassive. The little guy at the wheel grinned and said, "I am José, señor. If there is anything?"

"How long will it take to get ashore?"

"Possibly an hour. Your country's patrol planes search overhead watching for"—he waved a hand in our direction—"such as this. Ever since Señor Camino escaped your police and came here and when Professor Francisco Hernández was abducted on Señor Ortega's orders, they search."

"These aren't U.S. territorial waters," I reminded him.

"Neither is Cuba. There are, how you say, overflights for preventive measures. For that we are rather grateful. There are those who wish to flee this cursed place and your search plans have been useful to stopping pursuit and rescuing those attempting to escape."

"How many get away, José?"

"Very few, señor. It is regrettable. Carlos Ortega has many ways of preventing such democratic action." Very casually he glanced my way. "You are aware, of course, that he knows the Señor Morgan is coming with his wife."

"So I hear. He could have made it easier."

José shook his head with quiet emphasis. "No, señor. He would not wish to antagonize your country if it should be known as such. Not at this point, at least. He has far greater power over you when your entry is illegal. I hope you do not regret your decision to come here."

"There aren't many places left to go."

"True," José agreed, "but be careful. It is not a friendly place."

While we were talking, José had crowded the shoreline, skirting the beach until we picked up a narrow inlet that was nearly invisible in the tangled growth. Without hesitation he nosed the boat through the vegetation into a passable channel and wound around its contours for a half mile. At the far end were a dock and a large ramshackle building that had listed under the unrelenting pressure of years of offshore winds.

"It will not be long now, Señor Morgan," José said. "I have a car waiting to take you inland."

The city of Nuevo Cádiz raised its magnificence in the midst of squalor, a modern monument to graft, corruption and open gambling that made pre-Castro Havana seem archaic by comparison. Military personnel in flamboyant uniforms were everywhere, officers sporting sidearms in spit-polished leather holsters, the enlisted troops strolling casually, rifles slung over their shoulders, a constant reminder to the populace that control still came down through the chain of command. Police officers were unduly officious, doing little more than directing traffic, knowing how minute their authority really was and resenting it.

Kim and I both spotted a dozen well-known playboy types from two continents and a spattering of Hollywood celebrities, but the big-money people were the ones you ordinarily wouldn't pick out unless you could recognize the signs. For most, Nuevo Cádiz was an interesting stop on the Monte Carlo—Las Vegas route, one that had potential if the political wheels spun in the right direction.

I signed us in the Hotel Regis as Mr. and Mrs. M. A. Winters, feeling myself get a little tight at the stares Kim was drawing and some of the more audible remarks some of the other guests made, not thinking I caught their language. I played it straight and ignored it, wanting to keep the supposed language barrier an edge on my side if I needed it.

The bellboy took us up to a suite on the fifth floor, accepted the ten-dollar American with a toothy smile and bowed himself out the door. Kim went to say something, but I held up my hand, made a motion toward my ear and pointed to spots around the room. "Nice place," I said. "Good honeymoon spot. Like it?"

"Beautiful."

"Told you you would. Wait till you catch the nightlife."

"I'd rather go shopping. We cut out so fast I didn't bring a damn thing."

I grinned at her and nodded. While we were talking we had located two of the bugs planted in the living room and Kim picked up another in the huge bedroom. We didn't bother to strip them out. They would be a useful decoy if we wanted to plant an idea in their minds. The only place that seemed clean was the bathroom, so if we had anything to discuss we could do it there with the shower going. Nice, in one way of thinking.

"Come here, honey," I said. My tone had a bridegroom touch and she scowled uneasily until I made an impatient motion with my hand. She came into my arms slowly and I buried my mouth against her ear. "Play it cozy, sugar. They'll be expecting this so don't do anything that will make them think differently."

She nodded, her hair brushing gently against my cheek, smelling of some fine perfume. I tilted her chin up with the tips of my fingers, feeling those big wild eyes engulf me, then suddenly my mouth touched her mouth, and just as suddenly it wasn't just a touch any longer, but a crazy maelstrom that tried to suck me into its vortex.

With a trembling hand, she pushed me away, her breath caught in her throat for a moment. Soundlessly, but so I could read her lips, she said, "That wasn't . . . necessary."

I didn't have to be quiet about it. "Wonderful doll. You turn me inside out." Her face flushed a little and I grinned at her. "How about trying the nightlife here? Maybe we can pick up a few bucks at the tables."

"Or lose it. But I think . . . it's a good idea."

We took our turns in the shower, changed into clean cothes, then went out to the elevator. I gave Kim enough money to shop for both of us while I got the feel of the city, making arrangements to meet her at the tables downstairs in two hours. Given two people sensitive to the temper of a city, it wouldn't take too long to get the mood of the place. Kim would probe the locals, the salesclerks, draw them out the way one woman can another, and I'd tackle the tourist angle.

Although Nuevo Cádiz, the capital city of this politically volcanic country, wasn't especially noted for authentic tourists. The big men at the crap and roulette tables found it relaxing because all the wraps were off; hoods found it a convenient place to cool off if the heat was too much for them back home, provided they could pay the freight; the jet set reveled in the lush spas the government had erected and the Commies played their little games and waited to see which side to cultivate and harvest into their own world.

Looking out at the gaudy runways of the streets flanked by the glistening white façades of the hotels and casinos, it was hard to picture that four miles away on the tip of the peninsula was the graveyard of the living called the Rose Castle and inside was a man named Victor Sable and someplace in there I had to reserve a room for myself.

I tried my luck in four of the places, playing lackadaisically at the crap tables, picking up a couple of hundred bucks behind the shooters. It was still too early for the big action, most of the trade in catching the Las Vegas-style supper shows. But the mental climate was far from Vegas. There was something furtive about this place. It was subtle fear you could almost feel and smell, something in the attitude of the stickmen and croupiers. There were too many hardcases busily engaged in doing nothing except inspecting the crowd, noticeable bulges pulling their tuxedos out of shape, strangely military in their carriage, with hostile eyes their smiles couldn't conceal.

The most peculiar thing was the absence of the little people. Unlike similar cities, there were no shoeshine boys, no hookers working the bars, nobody trying to shake you down for a few coins on the street. What few I saw went about their business with their heads down and did it quickly. Twice, I deliberately approached them, ostensibly to ask for directions. One said he didn't speak English and the other simply pointed and held up two fingers for the blocks I had to travel, looked around him nervously, then scurried off.

When it was time to meet Kim I walked to a cabstand and asked the driver to take me to the Regis. When he pulled out from the curb I asked him, "When do things move around here, buddy?"

"Soon, señor. Once the heat of day has passed."

"Recommend anyplace special?"

His shrug said one place was the same as another.

"How about the games? They straight? I'd hate to drop a bundle on a rigged wheel."

This time his eyes caught mine in the mirror. "The government sees to it that all things are run honestly." It was like reciting a well-memorized line.

"Quite a place. What was it like before?"

Once more I met his eyes and they were a little cagy. "Very different, señor. There has been a great improvement."

"For the better?"

"Oh, si, señor. Much better now. There is no more poor. The government has seen to that." It was another pat line. I was wondering if he ever drove through the slum area that bordered all this opulence.

The gaming rooms of the Regis avoided the Las Vegas look. The effect was more of early-twentieth-century splendor, the place swathed in heavy draperies and thick velvet carpeting, presided over by huge crystal chandeliers whose prisms threw weird spectrums on the tables below. There was a Diamond Jim Brady atmosphere and you could almost hear the money rustle in the thick wallets of the patrons. Currency from a dozen countries was being changed at the counters into stacks of chips, and multilingual hostesses circulated with bubbling bottles of champagne. Dress was mixed between casual and formal, with money being the only common denominator.

I wasted a half hour losing at stud poker, then hit a streak and added seven hundred to my pot before I moved on. What I wanted to establish was the attitude of a restless newcomer trying on things for size before getting into anything big, not caring one way or another whether I won or lost. Either way, I tipped the dealers a big bite so they'd have me spotted for another go around before I tried another pitch.

Kim came in just before nine o'clock and joined me at the roulette wheel. Once again she got those looks, and murmurs of appreciation ran around the table and the envious eyes sized me up when she took my hand like a loving wife was supposed to. I could pick out a couple of them who would have tried a continental approach to making a play for her, but I was just a little too big and my face was the kind that said I wouldn't go for that bit at all without crippling somebody, so there were regretful shrugs and they went back to the game.

When I lost out on a dozen turns I took Kim over to the bar, ordered a couple of drinks for us and said, "How'd you make out?"

"Purchasing power buys a lot of things around here. Incidentally, I put everything upstairs."

"They shake the place down yet?"

"Thoroughly but efficiently. Ordinarily, you'd never notice it. They're very proficient."

"I expected that. What did you pick up?"

"A confirmation of our information," she said. "The government is nominally run by a president and his cabinet who were forced on the people by Carlos Ortega's machine. They're merely figureheads who have to do as they're told. It's the same old pattern. The people get a look at prosperity and have hopes of sharing in it, but it's all eyewash. Ortega controls the Army and they control the population. It all happened in a subtle takeover instead of a revolution, but it was just as effective."

"Then why doesn't Ortega just assume control?"

"Because he wants world approval, for one thing. He likes money and he likes power, but of the two, he'll take money first. He's got a gold mine going for him here and if ever the balance swings in the wrong direction he'll be able to get out with a fortune the very same way the other dictators did."

"But enough money and he can swing the power package too," I stated.

"Exactly. Right now the government funds are depleted because they overextended themselves on their building program. Domestic taxes are murderous and if it weren't for the hard course the Army takes there might be open rebellion."

"That won't work."

Kim shook her head and sipped at her drink. "I don't

know. There's a peculiar feeling running through the people I spoke to. They seem to like this figurehead president. Although he can't do anything, he's one of them and on their side. He's bucked Ortega twice and made it stick and my bet is that Ortega would have had him erased if it wouldn't have put him on the spot. Given one opportunity, or confidence that he'd be backed up by the right governments, and he'd pull the cork."

"That fits the Commie trend."

"I don't know. We backed them down in Cuba and they may not want to jeopardize their present status by going that far out for an inconsequential place like this. The other Latin American countries might toughen up at that. No, I think the Reds are playing it cute and waiting it out. If Ortega makes it on his own they'll side with him. If he falls, they'll bypass this situation."

"And that brings us to Victor Sable."

"Ortega's ace in the hole, Morgan. He can bargain with him. Both sides want him badly and Ortega's waiting until the price is right."

"Damn, we should have moved in with troops to start with."

"And risk a global war? Then the Commies *would* back up Ortega. They'd have the propaganda advantage for one thing and a ready-made secondary government to support him for another. Besides, it would give them the excuse to pull a power play in the other hot spots in Asia where the lines of communication favor them."

I finished the drink and waved the bartender over for a refill. "And old Morgan gets tapped to be the patsy."

"Somebody has to do it," Kim told me. "You were just a natural for the part."

"Gee, thanks, kid."

"No trouble at all," she smiled sweetly. "Consider it an education in global politics and a rebate on your jail sentence." She let the smile go wider, then suddenly grimaced when I kicked her shin with the side of my shoe.

She didn't stop smiling, but she did say, "Ow . . . you bastard."

"No trouble at all," I said. "Consider it an education in the art of learning not to push a man."

She let out a little laugh that was real this time and finished her drink with me. Behind us the crowd had picked up, standing four deep around the tables, and we went over and joined the throng. Had it not been for Kim, we couldn't have gotten through to the crap tables, but she

had the knack and the smile and found us a place, played
small bets with me until I got the dice, then stood beside
me when I let them roll.

Four times in a row I made my point the hard way and I
could sense the sudden interest in the players. The big
money started following my lead and the chips were piling
up in front of me. The stickman changed the dice, let me
inspect them; then I threw two sixes and did the same on
the next toss. A four went out and there was a small sigh
from the edge of the table and an apprehensive cough
from the guy next to Kim who was winning for the first
time that night. I rolled a nine and an eight with a dead
silence hanging around us; then the four turn up. The excited chatter turned into applause and the other tables
started to empty when the word spread that a lucky streak
was on.

Once more the stickman called for a pause and spoke
hurriedly to his assistant to run in fresh cubes. From behind me a voice with the hoarse quality of somebody who
cheered too wildly said, "They'll do anything to break
your luck, buddy."

I turned around and grinned at him. He was a dark-
haired guy with a lopsided smile and a face that had the
touch of an old pug. His eyes crinkled humorously so that
one seemed higher than the other and he had one hand
wrapped around a stack of black chips. The other one he
held out to me. "Marty Steele from Yonkers, New York,"
he said. "I'm playing right behind you. Keep it up."

"Morg Winters," I told him. "I'll keep trying."

"Those new dice won't do them any good. I can smell
it."

"You're better than I am. It's all the laws of chance."

"That's good enough for me." He grinned again, his
face twisting oddly, and let out a throaty laugh.

I got the new dice, warmed them in my hand, didn't
bother with a shake at all and tossed them out, watched
them bounce off the backboard and come up a seven. The
total silence erupted into a booming roar of delight as
everybody grabbed for their chips and I picked up the dice
again.

This time I rolled a three, but nobody was betting
against me. The table was loaded, the players watching me
expectantly, the stickman eyeing the way I handled the
cubes to make sure I wasn't pulling a switch, and to make
it easy for him I held them out in plain sight on the tip of
my fingers and made my roll. The first time I drew a five,

the second roll came up an eight and the third pass showed the three. It wasn't a lucky streak anymore. It was damn near a rout and the crowd knew it and yelled for more. Beside me Marty Steele was piling his chips up, his voice breaking with encouraging shouts.

But I had to disappoint them. I passed the dice and crammed the chips in my pocket and Kim's purse and waved off the others who were imploring me to continue. They thought I was crazy not to stay when the dice were hot, but I had been to the well often enough not to louse up a good thing. We cashed in the chips for twelve American thousand-dollar bills and I took Kim's arm and headed for the door.

She stopped me as we passed the ladies' room, told me she wouldn't be long and I said I'd meet her at the bar.

This time I was thirsty and ordered a beer, having it halfway finished when a softly throaty voice next to me said, "You're a stinker. I could have killed you."

She was a tall, sensuous blonde with penetrating brown eyes and a wickedly pretty smile, one manicured hand toying with a jeweled ornament at the bottom of the deeply cut V in the green-sequined evening dress that exposed the amber rise of full breasts. For a second I was too taken in by the daring expanse of skin she flaunted to say anything. She knew what she was like and had been told often and my reaction was expected.

"You should have kept playing," she said. "I was following you."

I put the glass down. "Win much?" It was all I could manage.

"Not enough. Not nearly enough," she laughed. Her voice had a distracting musical quality that could reach right out and shake you. "Are you going to play again?"

"Maybe. Right now I've had it."

"I wish you'd warn me when you're ready." She tilted her head and held out her hand. "I'm Lisa Gordot. I'm staying right here at the hotel. Your style of play is fascinating . . . almost domineering."

My hand wrapped around hers and twice while she spoke she exerted a gentle, inviting pressure. "Winters," I said. "What you saw was just fresh luck. It probably won't happen again."

Her eyebrows arched above her smile and the tip of her tongue showed between her teeth when she shook her head gravely. "I'm afraid you're not an inveterate gambler, Mr. Winters. There are some people luck seems to pursue forever. I have a strange feeling that you are one of them.

Ergo, I choose to pursue you. I assure you that I will be very relentless."

"That's not doing very much for my ego," I said. "The money or because of me?"

She took her hand away with deliberate slowness, her smile a rich promise of other things. "Let me say . . . the money *and* you." She stood there a few seconds, just looking at me, then smiled again and walked past me with slow, long-legged strides and the gown shimmering around her trim curves from the lights overhead.

I didn't even realize that Kim had come up beside me until she spoke with a curious bite in her voice. "Who was that?"

When I looked at her I made it as casual as possible. "Lisa Gordot. She was congratulating me on my lucky streak."

Kim's eyes narrowed in a frown. "So that's who she is," she whispered.

"What's that supposed to mean?"

"Your friend is a foreign national, a member of the jet set. She's upset two friendly governments by embroiling their members in sensational scandals, encouraged the death of the Saxton heir by having him duel over her and caused an Albanian diplomat's suicide when she laughed off his proposal of marriage. Nice people you know."

"Hell, I just met her," I said. "What would she want with me anyway?" Then I laughed at the little touch of animal jealousy that showed in her face and when she grinned back, said, "Come on, let's get out of here."

Outside, the street was ablaze with lights, the street heavy with traffic as taxis disgorged passengers in front of the casinos. Several blocks away the rectangular structures of the government-building complex were bathed in a pink glow, the fountains spouting multicolored streams of water. Workers on bicycles pedaled homeward wearily, never looking at the wealthy ones they served, completely submerged in their own problems.

Both of us were hungry, so we cut down a side street at the direction of a newsboy and picked out a restaurant nestled in an older row of buildings that catered to the ordinary public, and ordered a steak. By the time we finished, everybody else had left and the tired proprietor was glad to usher us out and lock the door.

That was as far as we almost got. I saw the shadows move across the street, shoved Kim sprawling and dived into the shadows behind her as the shot blasted out and the window behind us shattered into a spiderweb of cracks. I had the .45 in my hand trying to steady on a target, but nothing moved at all. I tapped Kim, pointed to a pile of cartons on the curb, waited until she moved in the lee of their protection, then jumped up and zigzagged across the street and flattened against the wall. Excited voices were beginning to shout inquiries from the windows above and somewhere a woman let out a shrill wail of despair.

I stood there for a full minute, then edged forward when my eyes adjusted to the darkness. But it was too late. An alley cut back and disappeared into the maw of the night and whoever had waited us out from that point had gone. My foot rolled on something by the wall and I picked up an empty .38 shell casing, smelled it, then flipped it into the gutter.

They didn't come in with sirens screaming. They just hit both ends of the street, turned down with their men hanging out the door, guns leveled, and stopped when they came to us. Before they spotted me I dropped the .45 and the extra clip behind a pile of trash just inside the alley and kicked some papers over it with my foot. We didn't bother to make a break for it. We simply went over and joined them. The lieutenant in charge gave me crisp instructions on how to stand with my hands up against the car, patted me down until he was certain I had no weapon, returned my wallet and pardoned himself to Kim. If he tried patting her down he was going to get creamed, but his better manners took over when he saw the look of outraged innocence on her face and he coughed into his hand. When he said, "Señor . . ." I spit almost at his feet and told him, "A hell of a place this is."

When the restaurant owner was sure everything was under control he came out shaking at the knees, complaining about his broken window and assuring the militia that we had done nothing except eat and immediately upon leaving had been fired upon. But the lieutenant had orders. We were to accompany him to headquarters and make a report, instituting a complaint if we wished and an investigation would follow. I gave the little guy in the white apron a hundred bucks for his window, made a friend, and told the lieutenant, "Let's go."

Russo Sabin was Director of Police. He was small and chubby with a moon face that had a built-in smile around a pencil-stripe moustache and glossy black hair that fitted his skull like a cap. He was so overbearingly friendly he rocked in his desk chair with his hands laced in front of his stomach like a happy Buddha. His eyes seemed to dance with the pleasure of being able to accommodate visitors to his country and he almost crooned with the delight of doing so.

But Art Keefer had said he was Carlos Ortega's hatchet man. I could believe it. Those laughing little eyes held more than pleasure. They had seen and enjoyed death too.

"Ah, yes, Mr. Winters. It is regrettable, of course, but in a way, almost to be expected. You might say, it was your own fault."

"My fault to be shot at?" I exploded.

He held up one calming hand. "You had an extremely large amount of money on your person. You chose to dine in a rather out-of-the-way place for the usual tourist, therefore making yourself a target for robbery. This was not the first or the last time such unfortunate incidents have occurred."

"Listen . . ." I started.

He cut me off again. "The hotels and casinos have accommodations so guests can deposit their winnings in a safe place. There are signs and instructions in several languages to that effect. Instead, you chose to ignore them. Probably some despicable person took note of your winning streak and departure, and followed you hoping to obtain your money. Naturally, we will investigate. If you will sign . . ."

"Forget it." I pushed the papers back across his desk. "It's too late now."

"Then there is little we can do. That is the law," he said. "Of course, I would like to caution you against a similar situation."

"Nice of you."

"Now, one more official duty." His smile brightened noticeably. "You have your papers, naturally."

"At the hotel," I lied.

"I see." He rocked back in his chair, still the genial host. "Perhaps you should send for them. Or if that is an inconvenience, my men could accompany you to assure your identification."

"Look . . . we're registered at the hotel. . . ."

"Ah, yes, we have checked that. But regulations being what they are . . . and certainly we wish to protect American nationals . . ."

I played the game to its limit. I shrugged and said, "Okay, if you want to louse up our evening." I reached in my pocket and thumbed off a pair of bills. "But if we can make it a little easier on everybody I'll be glad to oblige." I tossed the money down on the desk.

"Very generous, Mr. Winters. Of course we are not interested in discomforting you and your wife. We are here to serve. I'm sure the incident can be forgotten, but I might suggest that in the future your visa be available for inspection."

"Sure," I said, "we'll do that."

"Then my men will be happy to return you to your hotel."

"Never mind. I'll hop a cab."

"As you wish."

He was still smiling when he left, but his eyes were looking at the money.

In the cab Kim squeezed my hand. "You didn't fool him, you know."

"I didn't intend to. He'll just let the rope stretch out as long as he wants to."

"You think they set that up?"

"No."

"Why not?"

"Because everybody I've seen around who's armed is carrying a Czech-made automatic that fires a 7.65 millimeter bullet. The one who took a shot at us used a .38, firing standard U.S. ammo."

"Then it *was* a robbery attempt."

"Kid," I said, "you've been out of the field too long. A desk job has warped your thinking. A stickup is pulled at point-blank range, not from across the street. That was an assassination attempt."

"But . . . who?"

"I don't know. I'm even wondering just who he was aiming at. It could have been you."

She took it calmly, turning her head to look at me evenly. "Possibly."

Before we reached the hotel I had the driver turn down the street where we were almost nailed, hopped out, retrieved the .45 and got back in the cab. If this kind of thing kept up I didn't want to be caught without a rod.

I pointed to the hairline of light showing under the door and looked at Kim. She stepped to one side and shook her head, motioning with her hand that she had cut the switch before she left. I nodded, turned the knob and shoved the door open.

There were two of them there, a lean, swarthy character in an immaculate uniform wearing two rows of medals and a holstered gun at his side and lounging comfortably in the big chair, a thickset man in a black Italian silk suit whose soft smile was really no expression at all. His black hair was lightly touched with gray that almost matched eyes of the same color, a betrayal of nationality he must have hated because he deliberately shaded them with their lids to seem almost sleepy.

Danger was there in both of them. Overt in the one standing, impending in the other. But the edge was mine because I encompassed both types and let it show when I pulled Kim in behind me and closed the door with my foot.

"This is a private suite," I said.

The one in the chair didn't change his expression a bit. "Not exactly, Mr. Morgan. It is so only when we wish it to be."

"And who is that 'we' you're speaking of, Mr. Ortega?"

His eyes opened a fraction. "Ah, you know who I am then?"

"Don't play games with me," I said. "I'm no damn amateur." Kim's hand tightened on my arm. "What are you doing here?"

"That's what I came to ask you, Mr. Morgan. You see, I have investigated and find no record of your entry into our country. In fact, you have used an alias on your registration here."

I looked at him casually and shrugged as unconcernedly as I could. "So throw us out. I couldn't care less."

The tall guy behind Ortega frowned and stiffened. Carlos Ortega let his smile go a little wider and shook his head. "Oh, that won't be necessary. Naturally, an inquiry *is* in order since your entry is illegal."

"You have some fine sources of information."

"Yes, we do have that. My people are trained to recognize . . . ah, certain important persons." He waved indolently at the man behind him. "Major Turez here identified you immediately at one of the casinos."

"Nice of him. I understand you have a ship leaving for Rio tomorrow. We'll be glad to hop it."

Carlos Ortega spread his hands in amazement. "But why, Mr. Morgan? That is not the purpose of my visit. If I wished, I could detain you and hand you over to the American authorities. I am sure they would be happy to have you back there."

"Why, then?" I asked with a grin. My eyes flicked between the both of them and the major looked like a cat had scratched him.

Ortega said, "Our country has welcomed many people seeking . . . shall we say, political asylum? We are not concerned with your past, only that you are satisfied here and conform to our laws. That is not too much to ask, is it?"

"Suits me, but if you don't like the situation, I'll be glad to ship out."

"Perhaps you would be happier if you stayed. Your, er . . . wife would enjoy her honeymoon here."

My grin spread clear across my face and there wasn't any humor in it at all. The major's hand went to the gun at his belt and his fingers fumbled for the leather catch. One day all that rigging was going to get him killed. I said, "Ease off, you. You're looking at my *wife*, understand. We're legally married and anybody . . ."

And this time Carlos Ortega managed an expression. An apologetic one. "Please, Mr. Morgan. I know this, I know this. Georgia, it was, duly registered. I'm surprised you even took the chance, but legality I approve of. I am sorry if I offended, but in the nature of my work—"

I cut him short. "Okay, forget it."

"Certainly. Now that we've had our understanding, I may add that there are certain services this country might be able to offer you . . ."

"Like converting hot money into clean stuff at a discount?" I put in.

His nod was a generous one. "To be frank, it can be arranged," he said.

"I'll think about it."

Carlos Ortega stood up and I got a good look at him. In the chair his size had been deceptive; now I saw the brutal strength in him and knew the way he had forced himself into power. He wasn't the type many men could come against and live. He was all raw power with no concern for personal safety, giving himself over to some wild driving force inside himself that even he couldn't understand.

"Incidentally, Mr. Morgan, my associate, Señor Sabin, informed me you suffered an altercation of sorts recently."

"Somebody tried to kill me."

"Regrettable. I have given instructions personally to investigate fully. Would you have any idea who it could have been?"

"Your associate suspected a robbery attempt," I said.

Something changed in Ortega's face. "Not from across the street," he told me.

"That's what I figured."

He gave me an odd stare, then turned to the major and motioned for him to leave, then followed him past us with a stiff little bow to Kim. I opened the door, watched them step into the corridor, then turned on my nasty charm and said, "By the way, Mr. Ortega, would it inconvenience your people if I yanked the bugs out of the room? After all, it is our honeymoon."

It never fazed him at all. It was almost as if he had expected it. "Certainly, Mr. Morgan. I apologize for the clumsy installation."

So I laid it on a little thicker. "And I'd reprimand whoever shook the room down. They weren't very good either."

The major's face darkened with suppressed fury, but Ortega seemed to enjoy his discomfort. "It is very difficult when you deal with professionals, Mr. Morgan. Good night, sir, and congratulations to the señora."

I closed the door and looked at Kim. "That was quick."

She watched me carefully, curiosity in her face. "You pushed too hard, Morgan."

"I don't like reflections on my marital status, baby . . . such as it is."

She had the decency to blush, but her face didn't change any. "I didn't mean that. I was referring to the hidden microphones."

I grunted and went over to the sideboard and poured out a cold beer. "He didn't mind, kid. He would have thought me pretty stupid if I didn't spot them. Besides, something has him worried."

"Oh?"

"That shooting," I said. "He spotted the catch in it right away. He didn't kid about it. He wants me alive if he expects to nick my bundle. We got more here to worry about than the Ortega regime."

Kim took the glass I held out. "But . . . who else . . ."

"That's what I'm going to find out. So far I've only been pitched to once."

She didn't get the drift of my meaning so I finished my beer, put the glass down and told her I'd be back later.

6

Like las vegas, there was no night in Nuevo Cádiz. There was a brightly illuminated darkness, but not night. The carnival atmosphere grew more frantic, the crowd thicker, the noises louder as the hours passed. The play at the casinos was heavy and the ballrooms were crowded with couples and groups taking a break, but there was one thing that never changed, the harried bartenders sweating out their shift before their relief came on and they could go home.

At the Delmonico I slid on a stool, ordered Fleischmann's Preferred and ginger ale, passed a five-spot across the bar and told the guy to keep the change. He gave me a grateful nod and made my drink a double, then looked at my face again. "You been in before?"

"Just got here."

"States?"

I nodded.

"What's the news from home?" he asked me.

"How long you been away?"

"Too long."

"Then you haven't missed anything," I told him. "Nothing's changed. A few more buildings in Manhattan, a big LSD kick on and the same scramble for the buck."

"Better'n here, though."

"So go back."

He shook his head. "Can't. I jumped bail on an assault rap and they'd pick me up."

"Guilty?"

"Hell, yes. Why you think I skipped out? I put enough time behind the wall the first stretch." I got that funny look again. "Don't I know you?"

"I get around."

He grinned and mopped the bar down in front of me. "Yeah. Plenty of us here. Maybe it'd do better to serve time. When they got you on the hook here they tap you for everything they can. You clean?"

"Enough."

"Then stay that way. You don't know how rough it can get. These monkeys can look like jokers, but they got something rolling for them here and play it all the way. Get in on the action yet?"

"Picked up a few bucks shooting crap," I said. "Met some broad who liked my style. Called herself Lisa Gordot."

The bartender's head came up and his eyes had a sudden interested look. "You picked up more than a few bucks, then. That doll only goes after the long green."

"That's what I figured. I quit when I was ahead and she wanted me to play out the streak. What's with her?"

He refilled my glass and took the other five I handed him. I knew he was debating how far he could go with me, then he shrugged and said, "Just an idea I got, but some of the others seem to think the same thing. She's stranded here. Right now she's after running money." He made a funny expression with his mouth, then leaned on the bar close to me. "Stay away from that chick. She's trouble right down the line. She had a couple of chances to cut out, but our local Director of Police has tagged her for his personal property and is making sure she's gonna stick around."

"Russo Sabin?"

"For a guy what just got here you seem to catch on quick."

"I got to, pal."

"Then keep it in mind. That fat snake can get you killed as quick as look at you. Him and his crew don't take no interference with their pleasures. If you got a record back home, chances are he has a file on you in his office right now. Matter of fact, we're being watched right now, so if anybody asks you about our little conversation, tell 'em it was baseball. I'm a nut on the game, so play along. I like my job. It's better'n making license plates in a prison shop."

"Can do," I said. "But I'm still curious about the Gordot dame."

"Where are you staying?"

"The Regis."

"Check her out with Angelo, the bell captain." He squinted at me again, puzzled. "Damn, I know you, buddy. Got a name?"

"Down here it's M. A. Winters."

"What's it back home?"

I grinned at him. "Morgan the Raider."

"Damn," he said. "I'm talking to big time."

"Forget it," I said.

He laughed and filled my glass again. "Already did. Have one for the road."

The picture was taking on some queer little highlights. It could be that they were trying to box me in, but the reason wasn't clear yet. Lisa Gordot led to Russo Sabin; he led to Carlos Ortega and where they were leading to could be the forty million I supposedly had. The only hitch was the murder attempt. They'd know damn well I wouldn't keep that kind of cash where it could be grabbed very easily and I was smart enough to make it tough for them to find it if they went after it on their own. Then there was Ortega's attitude. He didn't like someone trying to knock me off either.

On the other side, there was still Victor Sable to consider. If, as the Washington boys suspected, he was playing footsies with the Reds, they would be in the picture too. Their own espionage network was big enough to suppose they could possibly have a dossier on Kim and if they played the obscure angles, might figure she was using me as a cover to get here with the hope of springing Sable somehow . . . or of knocking him off so they couldn't get their hands on him. The assassination try could have been for her.

It all sounded smooth enough until the other factor came in. Bernice Case was in the morgue and that was because I had started my own probe to run down that fat bundle of government money.

But there was something I could find out for myself if my lucky streak hadn't run out.

Lisa Gordot pinched a small stack of chips between her thumb and forefinger, her eyes watching the cubes flash across the dark green felt of the crap table. Twice she played the pass line, lost, then came back even when she dropped a couple on a field number. She had changed into a black sheath and had done something different to her hair, but this time there was no gaiety in her eyes and little worried lines touched her forehead as she scanned the table and the players.

I moved in next to her and without looking, said, "Still think I'm lucky?"

First, only her eyes moved, ready to cut me off, then

she recognized me and a smile brightened her face. It was the look of relief a drowning person has when he grabs a floating plank. It was there for only a second before she disguised it and it was something she never knew I read and understood, but it was my jungle too and I had been up too many trails and could spot all the signs.

"Well," she said blithely, "my benefactor has returned to the wars. I was beginning to think the laws of chance and not of fortune regulated this fascinating sport."

"It does," I told her.

She showed me her chips. "This says not."

"Want a system?"

"I thought you were brilliant enough to stay with your luck."

"Let's try the laws of chance first. I'll show you something."

"I'm willing to learn." She slid her hand through my arm and gave me an impish grin. "I'll try anything once."

"Like what?"

"What would you like?" The grin was still there.

"Let's stay with the dice first," I said. "How many times do the field numbers hit?"

Her eyebrows raised in thought a moment. "Not too often."

"Because the wipe-out numbers come more often. Now, wait until the shooter misses four field numbers in a row. From that time on the law of averages says the field will show. It may take a while, but give it a try."

"Play with me?"

"Why not?"

So we held our places and watched the game. It took thirty-five minutes, but the combination came up three times. The guy rolling the dice was fast enough to show the pattern and after four misses at the field we scored. Once we had to double to recover, but it came up good. I sweated out six passes to stretch it, laid six big chips on the longest odds on the table, laughed when it went into the pocket and laughed again when Lisa picked up the stack that was shoved her way.

"You're right, my wild friend. It's a winning way, but it can take a long, long time and they have limits here."

"Okay, so I'll take the dice."

Her hand squeezed my arm. "How did I ever find you?"

"Luck," I said. "Not law of averages."

A couple at the table remembered me from the last hot streak and it didn't take long for word to get around. I

threw two sevens and the big money came out with a bab-
ble of happy voices, everybody shoving to get their chips
on the table. Lisa let out a bright squeal of pleasure, let
everything ride behind me, chewed her lip when I was
making my points and was quivering with excitement by
the time I was on my fourteenth lucky roll.

But there was no fifteenth roll. The short, stocky man-
ager was there beside me smiling a sick, oily smile and
waved his hands out to the stickman and said, "I am
sorry, sir, this table is now closed."

The anguished moans and indignant voices all started in
at once, but he was adamant behind his smile and the pro-
tests went right past him. He gave me a short bow, still
smiling, and said, "Simply a house policy, sir. You may resume play at another table. Unfortunately, you have broken the bank at this one."

"Sort of blows my streak though, doesn't it?" I laughed
and threw the cubes back on the table. "Forget it. I got
enough for this time around. How about you, Lisa?"

She finished stuffing the chips into her handbag, picked
up two more handfuls, clutching them to her breasts, the
excitement like a fine sheen of sweat on her lovely face.
"Whatever you want, big man. Anything you want."

"Anything?"

"Anything."

I laughed again and reached for my chips. "Then let's
cash in and see how far 'anything' goes."

Lisa's totally uninhibited play had gotten her a little
over twelve thousand dollars. I had stayed on the conserv-
ative side and cleared three, but some of the others had
gone overboard too and cleaned up the bank at the table. I
stuck my cash in my pocket, but Lisa didn't want to carry
hers or leave it in her room, so she excused herself, went
to the desk and after a lengthy conversation with the
clerk, passed him several bills and put the rest in an enve-
lope for deposit in the safe.

Apparently she had paid off her bill, because the desk
clerk was full of smiles when he passed her the receipts. I
stood at the bar toying with a drink and watched her leggy
stride take her to me, her blond hair a golden, fluffy crown
she tossed as she walked. It was all there, the invitation,
the promise, the pleasure, the way she held her hand out
to me and squeezed when I took it.

"Lovely man," she told me. "My lovely Mr. Winters
and I don't even know your first name."

"Er . . . Morgan," I said.

"Morgan." She said it with a caress and squeezed my hand again. "You have made me a very happy person, Morgan."

"I'm sorry I didn't get to it sooner."

"You were in time. It was close, but you came just in time."

"Drink?" I asked.

"Must we here?" The tip of her tongue moistened her lip and her eyes crinkled at me. "I told you I was a pursuer. My suite is amply stocked with all the necessities to see the evening out."

"No obligations, kid."

"No obligations, Morgan." Her hand slid easily under my arm and her fingers eased the glass out of my hand. "Come."

I put a bill on the bar, grinned at her and walked to the bank of elevators across the lobby. Halfway there a jockey-sized bellboy intercepted us with an apology and said, "Señor Winters, there is a message for you at the desk if you wish to take it."

I nodded, excused myself for a second and followed the bellboy. The message wasn't at the desk. It came from his lips that didn't move at all when he said, "I am Angelo, Señor Morgan-Winters. Max has told me of you. He is the bartender you spoke to earlier. I wish to suggest to you that you be careful with the Señorita Gordot. Señor Russo Sabin has men who have already reported to him and at the moment he is in the patio bar."

"Thanks, buddy."

He faked the act by handing me a note that simply stated I was to call my room, took the tip and walked off while I crumpled the paper and went back to Lisa. "Trouble?" she queried.

"A business matter I have to take care of. I'll meet you upstairs."

"Room 310, Morgan."

I pushed the button, waited until the doors opened and ushered her into the elevator. To anyone watching I was simply saying good night to a friend. Then I went back to the bar where I nursed a few drinks through some conversation with the bartender and two tourists.

It didn't take long to spot the pair who had been detailed to keep me in sight. Even in tuxedos they had a certain military arrogance they couldn't conceal. When they were certain I wasn't noticing them, one went to the desk and picked the scrap of paper from the wastebasket I had

thrown there, scanned it briefly and threw it back. A wry
face and a shrug explained to his buddy that it was of no
consequence and I grinned at their reflections in the back-
bar mirror.

But there was another one I had picked up even earlier.
There was nothing recognizable about him or his actions,
as much as I could see. It was his position that bothered
me. A potted palm interrupted the planes of his face and
general configuration, but from where he stood he could
see me plainly enough if he wanted to. Apparently he was
watching the players at a roulette wheel, but at the same
time, could keep me under surveillance too.

Ordinarily, it wouldn't have bothered me, but my mind
kept referring to the one other time tonight my eyes had
picked up the same sort of self-camouflaging when I was
rolling the hot dice. I had been too busy to catalog the incident then, but now it came back to me.

I watched him covertly, making small talk with the
tourist, then saw him turn and walk away, the palm still
screening his figure. *Hell,* I thought, *I'm getting spooked
by nothing at all. How many others could be standing in
positions just as commanding as his?*

The tuxedoed pair watched me for another ten minutes,
then lost interest until I said so long to everyone and went
to the elevator. I gave my floor number to the operator,
knowing they'd watch the pointer above the doors or
check back with him later. When I got off I headed in the
direction of my suite until I heard the elevator doors click
shut behind me, then took the stairs down to the third
floor and knocked on the panels of 310.

She had made good use of the time. Her hair was
fluffed in a carefully touseled way, the blonde highlights a
stark contrast to the sheer black nylon negligee that
hugged her body with a static crispness. Behind her on the
table a bottle of champagne was cooling next to two glass-
es and the wall radio gave out the soft rhythm of a sensuous Latin tune.

With nothing more than a warm, direct look, she in-
vited me in, then shut and locked the door. "Intimate," I
said.

"It's supposed to be. Drink?"

"You pour. I want to use your phone." I picked up the
receiver, got Kim on the second ring and told her where I
was and if anybody called there looking for me, she was
to tell them I was in the shower and would ring them
back. Then she was to call me. I didn't want to explain

with Lisa listening, but I didn't want to take any chances on Sabin checking up on my whereabouts.

When she handed me the champagne, Lisa said, "Is it wise to tell your bride about your . . . present engagement?"

"You seem to know a lot about me."

"One hears many things in this place, Morgan. A woman can tell a lot of things about other women."

"I've a very understanding wife."

The champagne was cold and sparkling and I looked at her over my glass. "I hope the same thing can be said about your suitor."

Her glass stopped midway to her lips. "Oh?"

"Russo Sabin. I hear he considers you his property."

"So you hear many things too, Morgan."

"I make it a point when I'm interested in somebody."

"Then don't concern yourself with him. Russo Sabin is a . . . a pig. An animal." A touch of ice showed in her eyes. "He is difficult to discourage. Impossible. He is the one who . . ." She stopped there.

"Who what?"

"It is nothing," she said. I held my glass out and let her fill it again. She knew I was watching her, looked up and smiled ironically. "You probably have heard everything about me."

"Only in broad outline. I'm still interested."

"Why?"

"Because Sabin might have something going against me too."

Lisa put the bottle back in the ice and perched on the arm of a chair, one lovely leg swinging idly, unconscious of the way the negligee fell away from her thigh with each motion. "You are a strange person, Morgan. I don't know what it is, but you are something you are not supposed to be."

"Don't let it worry you."

"I'm not. It might be a help to me. So far you have been the only one that *has* been useful."

"Me and my lucky streak," I grinned.

"It will get me away from this damned place." A harsh tone gave her words a bite. "Since you are no doubt aware of my past, perhaps you really are interested in my present."

"Very much since it has Sabin in it."

She got up then, walked to the couch and sat down again, her crossed legs showing the same contempt for clothing. "I came here originally as a tourist," she said. "In reality, I was escaping certain consequences . . . legal action a government wanted to take against me. They would very much like to have me back to make a public scandal that will embarrass the opposition party. At least here I was safe for a while. I was hoping to find a . . . ah, sponsor who would enable me to eventually reach South America, but made the mistake of attracting the attention of Señor Sabin. He has made sure no such sponsor appeared." She sipped her drink and moved her shoulders in a small shrug. "That left me only the laws of chance at the gambling tables to finance my plans."

"And you couldn't beat the odds," I put in.

"Quite. The odds were all in Señor Sabin's favor. He has waited me out, knowing I was rapidly becoming impoverished. His attempts to force his attentions upon me have been increasing. He knows very well that sooner or later I will have to capitulate in order to survive."

"Then I came along."

"Exactly."

I hooked a chair with my foot, dragged it close to her and slouched in it. "That bundle you picked up tonight should get you clear, kid."

She gave me a wistful smile. "No, I'm afraid not. You see, when I get to my destination there will be certain parties with government influence that will have to be . . . paid off. That will take a good deal more. About fifty thousand dollars more."

"How long can a lucky streak hold out?"

She put the glass down and lounged back, watching me with sleepy eyes. "I have a great deal of confidence in yours, Morgan. You are very lucky for me."

"Then maybe you can help me stretch it."

"Just ask."

"You may not like it. Play Sabin along a little. He has me spotted with you. See if he has anything on me and what he's interested in."

"He might make some trouble for you."

"I'll worry about that later. Right now I want an inside track on that guy."

Lisa frowned, thinking. Then: "But if he thinks you are interested in me . . or I am in you . . . then he will find a way to make you leave and my luck will be gone."

"Don't count on it, baby. I'll make sure it rubs off on you. There are other ways beside a crap table."

For several seconds she didn't say anything. Then she

held out one graceful arm and said, "Come here, Morgan."

I got up and walked to the couch, put my glass down and reached for her.

She shook her head, slowly and deliberately. "Wait." I watched while she stood up slowly, yanked at the sash that held the negligee shut, saw it flare open with a motion of her arms and fall to the floor at her feet. She was naked and beautiful, lithe as a young tree, but molded with superb artistry from the high rise of her breasts to the sloping channel of her stomach.

My fingers gently traced the soft curve of her body just once. Just so briefly it was almost to see if she were real or not, and that was as far as it went.

Behind me Kim said, "Damn you!" and exploded across the room going for Lisa like a cat coming out of a bag and I grabbed her in an armlock and held her so tightly she couldn't move. She was too mad to do anything but hiss between her teeth.

Lisa had never moved. She watched it all with an amused smile, then let her eyes dart to mine. "I think you had better take your bride home, Morgan. I can't blame her for being angry. But you had better not lock her in a closet. She seems to have a way with locks."

"She's an expert," I said.

I let her stalk across the room rubbing her arm where I had twisted it, watched her build a drink and toss it down too quickly. "Okay, Kim," I said, "What was that act for?"

She spun, facing me with a white face full of anger. "We're not here to play games, you idiot!"

"How do you know what I was playing?"

"What do you call it, Morgan? Standing there with a bare-assed broad ready to trip you up and beat you to the ground. That's all we need . . . all we need to knock this whole package flat on its back. We gave you credit for having more sense . . . at least to pick *anybody* better than that . . . that piece!"

"Who do you suggest?" I said flatly.

Both of her hands were clenched into fists, her shoulders heaving with her heavy breathing. She never heard what I said. "Not a damn thing on . . ."

"You could have knocked, baby. You didn't have to pick the lock. You gave away more of the show with that bit than I did."

Her eyes glared at me. In the light from the single lamp her teeth were an even flash of white in the scarlet frame of her mouth and she looked like a beautiful panther ready to pounce. "This isn't going to be a favorable item in my report. From now on you're not getting any leeway from me at all."

"I can act on my own volition, kitten. They told you that too."

Her voice was a soft, deadly purr. "Only if I prefer it to be that way, Morgan. There won't be any more nonsense like this. And of all people, Lisa Gordot."

"I asked you before. Who do you prefer?" I took a step forward, slowly, then another, until I was right in front of her. Almost imperceptibly she moved back.

What she saw on my face made her drop her hand to her side where she kept the gun and I shook my head. "I could take it away again, girl. I could even get to mine first if that's the way it had to be played out."

She stiffened and her eyes got cold again. "You could only try."

"Not so, girl. You wouldn't use it on me anyway. If you had you would have gone for me instead of Lisa just a few minutes ago." I grinned at her then. "Thanks."

Puzzlement changed the expression on her face. "What for?"

"Being jealous, my lovely wife. Downstairs you were just plain jealous. Now you're trying to justify it."

Her hand never landed on my face as she intended it to. I grabbed her wrist again, twisted and jerked her to me and wrapped my fingers in the midnight sheen of her hair all in one motion. The startled gasp that rounded her mouth blended into a kiss that went wild with the suddenness of an explosion and turned into a shudder of pure delight as she felt me flip open the buttons of her blouse.

Resistance was a thing that melted like wax in a flame. There was no awareness of anything I did except taste her lips and merge us both into a caldron of passion that was so intense it was almost unreal. Then the last shred of nylon dropped from her while she stood on her toes, arms around my neck, her mouth fierce against mine while I kneaded the firm contours of her body.

I pushed her away from me, waited until she opened her eyes, then hated myself for doing what I did. I let a laugh crease my face and said, "See?"

For a moment she stood there unbelievingly, then she glanced at her clothes and herself and a slow flush crept into her cheeks. This time I didn't stop her when she let me have the open hand right across my cheek.

She walked to the bedroom, the fury high in her. I said, "It's part of being a pro, kid." Then she slammed the door in my face.

7

DAYBREAK was the deathwatch of Nuevo Cádiz. Down stairs some of the habituals would still be drifting between the tables, eyes red-rimmed from lack of sleep and their minds blurred with too much alcohol, but the rest of the world outside had buried itself, like Count Dracula, away from the morning sun. Across the stillness a rooster crowed shrilly, and annoyed at the lack of response, did it again.

I had awakened abruptly, fully conscious of being on the couch with the .45 warm in my hand. It had been an automatic reflex developed from years of waiting and watching, of hearing even when your brain was deep in the black of sleep. Inside the closed door of the bedroom I heard Kim toss restlessly, but that wasn't what had awakened me.

Then I heard it again, the slow tread of footsteps going past my door, the fractional hesitancy when they were directly opposite it. I slid off the couch, cocked the .45 under my arm so the click would be inaudible and crossed to the door in my stocking feet.

I waited, listening, then yanked the door open and jumped through it, the rod in my hand swiveling with my body, and I crouched to cover both ends of the corridor.

Nobody was there.

As quietly as I could, I ran to the elevator, tapped the button and heard the slow whine begin from far below as the car inched upward toward me. Whoever had been there didn't use the elevator. There wouldn't have been time for it to make the trip. But the stairwell was handy and the door still hadn't fully closed on its hydraulic cushioner.

Maybe I could have been getting spooky again, but somehow it didn't just have that feeling. I got back to the room before the elevator reached the landing, closed and locked the door and went back to the couch. All I could think of was that there were more games being played in Nuevo Cádiz than the ones downstairs.

A little before noon I heard the shower going and knew Kim was up. I let out a silly laugh because I knew a lot of ice had to be thawed before the tension was off the spring, so I did the same bit with the door lock she had done with Lisa's and let myself into the bedroom.

When I stepped into the shower with her she let out a stifled scream and would have slipped on her butt if I hadn't grabbed her. "So shoot me with the soap," I told her.

"You . . . get out of here!"

I squirted a mouthful of water over her. "Don't talk like that to your legally wedded husband, sugar. You might get your tail paddled." I took the soap from her fingers and began scrubbing her back. She tried to get away all right, and yelled a little, but what can a dame do when she's trapped in the shower by her husband anyway?

The ice cracked, but didn't thaw.

When I threw her a towel she deliberately turned her back, but I didn't give a hoot about modesty and whistled while I dried, flipped the towel over her head and walked out to get dressed. A screwy marriage like this had to have some compensations.

I didn't hurry at all. I loafed my way all the way into my shirt and tie before she finally gave up and came out with the towel wrapped around her like a sarong and stood there, daring to make a move.

"Sexy," I said.

"Shut up and get out of here. I want to get dressed."

"Rape or seduction, honey?"

"Neither." Her voice was like a knife.

"The game's getting rough, isn't it?"

"You warned me once," she said. "It won't happen again."

I looked at her and I wasn't smiling any longer. Very softly I told her, "I know it won't. It will never happen again. Not that way, my beautiful wife. The law allowed me certain privileges. Normal male ego imbues me with certain desires I might be challenged to fulfill. I'm wondering how it works the other way around."

"You'll never know."

I finished knotting my tie. "Oh, *I* know, honey. I'm curious about how long it's going to take *you* to know." I picked the .45 from the dresser, checked the load automatically, put it on half cock and stuck it in my belt. Then I looked at her in the mirror and said, "Things are beginning to jell out. Let's get the show on the road." I

left her there and went back to the living room and turned
on the radio. The tail end of a weather broadcast mentioned
a tropical disturbance building up five hundred miles
southeast of us that had possibilities of developing into a
hurricane.

She was able to play the game without any trouble. We
were tourist imports fresh enough to find things interesting, but jaded enough to steer clear of the traps. Kim and
I had sensed the tails the minute they had picked us up
when we left the hotel, the one behind us and the two in
front of us. It was a team operation and when they broke
off to let another pair do the shadowing we grabbed them
too and made it easy for them.

I had gotten a map of the local layout from the desk
that laid out the tourist attractions, and we hit each one
systematically and in bored fashion, not spending too
much time sight-seeing, but relieving the strain by popping
in and out of the bars that fed on the trade. At least our
tails were enjoying the hike if they were on an expense account.

All I wanted to do was establish a pattern.

By four in the afternoon the early floor shows broke out
their tired strippers and worn-out jokes and we spent more
time in these places than any of the others. By the time we
had hit the Orino Bar it was almost an accidental stop and
not a deliberate one, but we made a show of studying the
menu pasted on the window, decided to try the local food
and went on in. It was the first time we had eaten all day
and the two mock drunks behind us in the white suits the
businessmen wore were glad to see us pick a table, sit
down and order.

The Orino Bar wasn't like the others. From all appear-
ances it was an established institution patronized by the
residents. Native stone and timber had gone into its construction and time had weathered it until it had a flavor of
old Spain itself. The waiters were elderly and gracious, the
single bartender across the room a heavy-set man with an
archaic white moustache and two medals pinned to his
jacket. When he walked he limped, and when he looked,
he watched. His eyes barely touched us, then focused on
the pair in the white suits, hardened a little until he caught
the direction of their seated positions and watched us with
another degree of interest.

And now the pattern had to be set.

Three drinks for me did it. I insisted the waiter have one

with us, sent another to the bartender who mixed them so admirably and waved back his thanks when he saluted me with his drink. A little old man sitting by himself over a bowl of chili got a bottle of wine that lit his face up with a multitude of *"gracias."*

Then the show came on and the pattern was formed and I was getting drunk. They thought.

A four-piece orchestra had set itself up to the left of the small stage, a soft combo that lent a Spanish flavor to every piece it played. After the third number I sent them a bottle of champagne and got a "thank you crazy American" smile from all of them.

There were only three acts, a tenor soloist, a mediocre magician who relied more on his dirty jokes than on his feats for the applause, and a fiery, dark-skinned blonde blues singer, named Rosa Lee, with a body so fully in bloom it looked about to burst. She wore a two-piece halter and full skirt outfit, and when she whirled in tempo to the music the skirt flared out to show the loveliest pair of dancer's legs I had seen in a long time.

This one the crowd didn't want to let go and Kim and I were finished dinner and went into another round of drinks while she was still going.

And then she went into an old number called "Green Eyes."

Kim saw my sudden interest and leaned toward me. "What is it?"

"Our contact."

"How do you know?"

"The song. Art Keefer and I use it as a recognition signal. Something left over from the war when that band of us were working behind the lines."

"Nostalgia?"

"No," I said, "just habit. It's one of the things you never forget."

Kim gave me a small smile. "Your Rosa Lee was never in any war. She couldn't be over twenty-five."

"Art has her set up here for his own business."

"And would that be something like yours . . . stealing forty million dollars?"

I could feel my jaws go tight. "Knock it off, Kim. What he does is his own business. I told you he had nothing to do with that job."

"Tell me about the others."

"I thought you checked them out," I said nastily. "Your

Intelligence figured him for being killed, so they can't be too damn bright."

"Perhaps they never had any reason for suspecting otherwise."

"They didn't. Art just prefers it that way."

"Two others were reported dead too," she insisted.

I reached for my drink and put half of it away before I said, "Carey got it in an explosion. There wasn't enough left of him to identify. Art and I saw him go and they had to take our word for it. Malcolm Hannah couldn't outrun a train on a bridge he was blowing and went down with the wreckage and a couple of thousand other bodies in the Nazi troop movement."

"And Sal Dekker?"

"Caught and imprisoned in a concentration camp. Tortured but was unable to reveal any future operations because we never knew about them until we were briefed prior to their execution. He escaped, got tangled in a land mine, was badly hurt, but lucky enough to be rescued by some friendly farmers and turned over to Allied forces just as the war ended. He spent a few years in an Army hospital, then went to Australia."

"So you *could* have had help," Kim said. She wouldn't let the thing alone.

"Not Dekker, sugar," I told her. "He was the only one of us who truly hated the whole business. We enjoyed every minute of it. All he wanted to do was be a farmer. He's got that now."

"But that brings us back to you."

"How about that?" I said.

On the stage Rosa Lee had come to the end of her routine in a burst of applause. I waved the waiter over, showed him the magic in a ten-dollar bill and asked him to invite the little lady to our table for a drink.

The bill went into his pocket while he told me that ordinarily the performers didn't share the guests' tables, but since the señorita was present it would possibly be all right and went away to get her. All the booze I had been buying for everybody else made the request look like a standard American habit anyway, so watching Rosa Lee hip-swinging to our table didn't come as a surprise. Another two bottles of champagne to the orchestra kept them playing happily and loud enough to drown out our conversation.

"Rosa Lee," I said. "My wife Kim, and I'm Morgan . . . Winters. Sit down. You were pretty good up there."

She tucked her skirt under her and slid into the chair I held out for her.

"Drink?"

"Manhattan, please."

I passed the order on to the waiter and toasted her with my glass. "Liked your song 'Green Eyes' up there. Nice style."

Her eyes came alive. "Really? Strange that you should enjoy such an old number."

"I have a friend that likes it too. Art Keefer."

"I see."

The waiter placed her drink in front of her and she tasted it, approved, and took a bigger sip. I said, "Has Art alerted you?"

"Yes. What is it you need?"

"Access to a radio transmitter."

"I live at 177 Palm Drive. A transmitter and receiver are installed in the area over the garage in the back. Anything else?"

"Information from the States. A check on a dead woman named Bernice Case. Have Art contact Joe Jolley, who may have something on it by now. Tell him it's urgent and to expedite. Got it?"

"Clear."

"Now, is there any word going around about Victor Sable?"

"The one in the Rose Castle?" Her face drew into a serious expression when I nodded. "It isn't wise to ask questions about that one. For some reason he is in a special section under maximum security, a new place just built."

"How would you know?"

"A guard . . . a cousin of a friend of mine. He was drunk and boasting one night and mentioned it. This Sable . . . he is important enough to be under the personal attention of Carlos Ortega. All the guards in that section are personally responsible to him."

"I'll want somebody who knows about the new modifications to the prison."

Rosa thought a moment, then bobbed her head. "There is one who can be bought. The cousin of my friend, a Juan Fucilla."

"That could be trouble. If we could buy him he could sell out to somebody else."

"Only at the risk of his life, señor. He will be made to understand that."

"All right, I'll take your word for it. Set up a meeting with him as soon as possible."

"Tonight? Say ten o'clock?"

"That will be fine. Where?"

"Perhaps it had better be at my house. By then I will have contacted Art Keefer with your message and the transmitter will be available if you wish additional information." She paused and studied my face. "The Rose Castle, señor . . . it is virtually impregnable."

"How tight is the security?"

"Impossible to break without a direct attack by heavy forces. Even then, they have orders to kill Sable if such a thing occurs." She looked down at her hands as if studying her fingers. "Tell me, is this the reason why you are here?"

I said, "Yes," and Kim's hand tightened on my forearm in warning. I shook it off gently. "Rosa's on our side, kid. We can't play this in the dark."

Rosa agreed with a nod. "You are . . . agents?"

"Of a sort."

"This is a priority mission?"

"Top."

"We will do everything possible if it means we may be able to overthrow this regime."

"How many people have you got available?"

"Key government people are in hiding. About two dozen are trained and experienced in the military phases of what may be done. We have deliberately kept the force small to avoid infiltration and for mobility. The people, of course, cannot be counted on until there has been a definite success by our group, then they will rally. At the moment they are kept in fear by Ortega's mercenaries."

"And the Commie influence?"

"They are waiting. We are not yet important enough to risk an international incident, but if they can move in subtly, they will, of course. Ortega has been cultivating them."

"When are you planning to move?"

Rosa's smile had a wry twist to it. "Whenever a situation arises that will unite the people and force the dictatorship out. That is why we are willing to cooperate with you."

I nodded. "We'll try to give it to you," I said. "One other thing . . . Art Keefer train your military group?"

"Personally."

"Good. I know his routine. I figured as much."

"One thing more, señor. You are being watched at this moment. They are Ortega's men under the command of Russo Sabin."

"Yeah, I know. I hope they enjoyed their dinner."

She stood up then, shook hands with us both and

walked away smiling, saying hello to some of the regular customers on the way. For another half hour I played the good-time Charlie, left a fat tip for the waiter and paid the bill. On the way out I swayed a little, said so long to everybody around, laughed at their good-natured replies and even went to the trouble of including Ortega's men in the fun and watched them smile back uncomfortably.

Outside, we caught a cab and when I leaned back against the cushions Kim looked at me curiously and said, "What's the matter?"

"There was something funny back there."

"Oh?"

"I made a big enough ass out of myself to get everybody looking at me."

"You succeeded admirably."

"Not quite."

Kim frowned and waited.

"One made quite a point of *not* looking at me," I said.

They had done a better job of shaking the room down this time. Both pieces of thread I had used on the suitcase to tell if it had been opened were seemingly untouched, but they had missed the third gimmick, a tiny splinter of metal on the lock itself that was straightened out when it was flipped up.

Kim waited until I lifted the leather facing on the bottom of the suitcase and extracted the Miami bankbook and the safe-deposit-box key before she asked, "You think they found them?"

"Sure they did. They'll duplicate the key and forge my signature."

"If it was too easy they'll begin to suspect something."

"I doubt it," I told her. "We haven't been here long enough to stash something away with any degree of surety. The bag was specially made to hold this stuff and it was a good stunt. Ordinarily, nobody would have uncovered it."

"At least it will give us a little more time if they fall for it."

"We can't afford to wait, baby. Don't play these guys down. Ortega will have me hooked good when he finds out this is a decoy."

"How do you plan to move?"

"I'll know in the morning. Tonight I'm going to see this Juan Fucilla and get the new layout of the Rose Castle and find out what's turned up on Bernice Case. You're going to stay here. . . ."

"I am not!" she exploded.

"Knock it off. You'll do what I tell you to. This is supposed to be a honeymoon and newlyweds don't go prancing off all the time. There are other things expected of them."

"But . . ."

"I'm taking another exit out. Nobody will see me go out or come back. If anyone checks this room I want somebody here. If they ask for me, tell them I'm indisposed."

Her expression was a little too calculating. "Don't try taking a powder, Morgan."

I slammed the suitcase shut and stood up. Before she could protest I had her in my arms and tilted her face up with my fingers and kissed the end of her nose. "With a bride like you waiting for me? Hell, I'm looking forward to my husbandly due."

A call to Angelo brought us two magnums of champagne and an oversize plate of canapés to precede the supper I ordered. If there was a watch on our activities the indications would be that we'd be spending the rest of the night in the room behaving as a honeymooning couple should.

Without asking questions, Angelo described the way to get out the back entrance with the least risk of being seen. It involved a circuitous route used only by the hotel engineer and maintenance personnel, ending with an exit through the building that housed the central air-conditioning unit.

A foxy little smile creased his face when he finished and he added matter-of-factly, "You are here for something good, señor. That is so."

"Don't make me admit it." I grinned at him. "I have a reputation to protect."

"Yes, I know of that. It is more that I can sense a person's motives. Perhaps because I am of no consequence people pay no attention to a bellboy. I can study them at my leisure and understand their compulsions. I have reason to hate many people, señor. In Nuevo Cádiz I have opportunity to see and study the most extreme types."

I looked at him a little surprised. "Coming from a bellhop . . ."

"A university-graduate bellhop, señor," he said simply. "Student of political science. Someday, perhaps . . ." and he let it drop there.

I nodded. He didn't have to say any more. Angelo was

one of the little ones held in readiness. Carlos Ortega was
grossly underrating his opposition. He waved off the bill I
offered him and left with a polite little bow.

Kim's voice had no trace of antagonism in it when she
said. "You have the touch, Morgan. How do you reach
those types?"

"Why?"

"Because they trust you."

"Don't you?"

She looked at me a moment, her face bland. "I have to,
don't I?"

"Not necessarily. Why should you?"

"That's what annoys me," she said. "There's no patriotism behind your actions. There isn't even the motivation
of having your prison sentence reduced. It's only a game
to you. You're enjoying yourself. You're being Morgan
the Raider again, spoiling everybody else's pie. That's it,
isn't it?"

I swung around and picked up my jacket. "No."

"Then what is it?"

"If I told you, you wouldn't believe me."

"Try me."

"Why?"

"Because I'm the only one who hates you enough to understand it."

"Don't push me, baby."

"I'll push you as far as I want to."

"And one day that will be too far for you to reach me,"
I said.

Before she could answer I was out the door, heading for
the service exit Angelo had described.

He had chosen the route well. Only twice did I see anyone, a maid and one of the room-service boys, but neither
spotted me and I got into the basement, followed the line
of blue lights that barely illuminated the passageway to the
outbuilding, felt my way past the humming machinery
that threw a waterfall onto the roof overhead and found
the door that led outside. It had a one-way latch, so I gimmicked the tongue of the lock with the cover from a
matchbook so I could get back in and stepped out into the
darkness outside.

Somehow everything smelled different this night. It was
like those other nights overseas a long time ago when the
sense of smell had greater implications than the simple
tasting of odors. You could smell an abstraction then, a
danger that hovered in the air like a live thing. I could

smell it now too. It was too nebulous to define, but it was there. It wasn't as real as those other times, not as sharp or as imminently deadly, but it was waiting like a slow-acting poison and barely discernible.

I stood in the shadows, watching the other shadows. For thirty minutes I was motionless before I was certain I was alone, then I picked my way into the stream of pedestrian traffic, got off the main street and walked until I spotted a cab disgorging its passengers and waved it down.

Earlier I had checked the city directory and picked a spot two blocks from Rosa Lee's house. I gave the driver directions in his own dialect and he made a *U*-turn and drove off with barely a nod. Ten minutes later he pulled to the curb, took my fare and let me out.

Her house was a simple frame affair set back in a jumble of weeds that sprouted among the trees, the single lighted window hardly visible from the street. I picked my way up the path, waited until the headlights of an oncoming car had swept by, then climbed the rickety porch and knocked on the door.

Inside, the light went out before I heard the latch click and the door open. I said, "Hello, Rosa."

"Come in, Señor Morgan."

She pulled the curtains closed before she turned the light back on and I had a chance to look around. Shoddy as the place was outside, the woman's touch showed here. Rosa caught my casual glance and said, "We who live here are not permitted many luxuries, señor."

"The casino operations should eliminate taxes," I told her.

The shrug she gave me matched the cynicism in her voice. "Señor Ortega prefers to keep the people subject to his will. That way his occasional gratuities make him seem like a benevolent person."

"You should have done something before this."

"Have you noticed the military?" she asked derisively. "They were field hands, the uneducated, criminals. Now they are in positions of authority and carry out Señor Ortega's orders to the letter. There was a parallel in Germany when Hitler first took over."

I nodded. "Yeah."

She watched me closely. "Perhaps their time is at hand."

"Perhaps," I said. "Did you contact Art Keefer?"

"Yes. He will be monitoring the frequency right now. I gave him your message." She looked at her watch. "I suggest you call him immediately." She turned on her heel and glanced back over her shoulder. "This way, please."

The transmitter was a cleverly contrived affair some master craftsman had built into the hand-hewn beams that supported the old carriage house she referred to as the garage. It was so carefully concealed it would have taken a team of pros a week of working a specific area search pattern to locate it, and even then they'd have to have luck on their side. The manually extended antenna rose through a core in the beam and power was supplied to the unit through the house current. Rosa indicated the four supposedly beatup storage batteries haphazardly scattered around and told me they were on full charge for emergency use in the event of a power failure. Old car parts and a few discarded wheels gave the place an authentic appearance of an unused garage in case of a cursory search.

I switched the set on, dialed the frequency and turned up the receiver. "No longer than five minutes, señor," Rosa advised. "The government keeps a full crew monitoring the channels. We can't afford to have this position triangulated."

My hand waved the okay and I fiddled with the dial to break through the static, then picked up Art on the old Kissler code. Rosa listened, a frown on her face, not understanding what I was saying, nor would anybody else, but Art got it, all right.

"Morgan," I said.

"Go ahead, kid."

"You reach Jolley in New York?"

"Affirmative," Art said. "You started something up there. The guy's shaking in his shoes, but he came through."

"What's the pitch?"

"All he did was nose around trying to pick up something on Bernice Case and Whitey Tass. Someplace along the line he made inquiries about Gorman Yard and the squeeze started. Joey Jolley recognized it as coming from Whitey Tass and right now he's ready to cut out. He has something more, but he's holding out for protection. I had to play it by ear, so I clued him in on how to get to me. If he makes it I'll hold him here until you can speak to him."

"Did he say what he knew?"

"He hinted at it," Art told me. "Seems like he knows why Gorman Yard was bumped off."

"Damn!" I exploded.

"He'll be lucky if he can dodge Whitey Tass. I reached

a couple of my own contacts who told me something has Tass excited enough to call in all his troops on this movement. Now, where do I go from here?"

"Get Jolley and hang onto him," I said.

"Will do. Things okay there?"

I caught Rosa's signal of tapping her watch impatiently and said, "Shaping up. I'll call back."

"Roger and out," Art told me and switched off. I cut the power, flipped the dial off the frequency and put everything back the way it was.

Outside, the smell was just the same. The *thing* was there. I closed the door and turned around. "Juan Fucilla," I said.

"In a few minutes," she said. "It was difficult, but he will be here."

"Sure?"

"Positive. He smells money."

"What did you tell him?"

Rosa looked at me with a knowing little smile and said, "Money, of course. The love of which is the root of all evil."

"Who am I supposed to be?"

"One of the many persons interested in supplying forbidden items to the inmates of the Rose Castle. It is a flourishing business here, señor."

"Anything specific?"

"The usual. Tobacco, alcohol, narcotics. The smuggling of messages. It is a profitable arrangement for the guards."

"If they're caught?"

"Nobody bothers to investigate. It is the accepted way of things. Corruption breeds corruption. Since everyone is involved it is unlikely that they are interested in upsetting the system." She glanced impatiently at her watch again. "He is due here momentarily."

As if on cue, a heavy hand banged on the door. Once again, Rosa doused the lights, admitted her visitor and turned the lights back on again.

Juan Fucilla was a short, swarthy man in his late forties, with a shifty, predatory expression creased into the folds of flesh around his eyes. There was a touch of official impertinence in the way he acknowledged the introduction and slid into a chair. He pulled a silver case from his pocket, studiously ignored me and poked a vicious-looking black cigar between his thin lips and lit the end of it.

"Now, señor," he said, "Rosa tells me you have business to discuss."

I let a good ten seconds pass before I answered him so he'd get the message. At the end of it he licked his lips nervously and fidgeted with the cigar. I said, "If I have to go over your head, forget it."

His smile of assurance was as quick as it was phony. "You have to look no further, señor. I can make all arrangements. . . ."

"What's the bite?"

He started an eloquent shrug but I cut him off. "Don't give me any crap, buddy. I'm not here to dicker. Just lay it on the line. If I like it, maybe I'll go for it. If not . . . there are other ways."

My tone wiped the indignation out of his voice. He shrugged again, this time with resignation. "Usually it is fifty-fifty, señor. . . ."

"But this time it will be sixty-forty with me on the big end."

"But señor . . ."

"When I take the risks I get the big chunk. Once the deal is made and anybody tries to pat me down I guarantee they get hurt. This isn't amateur night. Now, do we take it from there?"

Fucilla grunted through his cigar smoke and nodded. "You drive a hard bargain, but perhaps it can be a profitable one after all." He looked at me through narrow eyes. "You can supply what is necessary?"

"Anything," I told him. "What's in demand?"

"At the moment there is a shortage in certain . . . narcotics. Other markets bring higher prices, so naturally there is a shortage here. If you can arrange . . ."

"Where does the money come from?"

His fake smile held a lot of meaning. "Most of those in the Rose Castle are political prisoners, señor. Naturally, they come from families of wealth who have since left for other areas. However, they do pay for . . . shall we say, requirements of those who were left behind?"

"The picture's clear. One more thing. How were they addicted?"

He didn't try to shake it off. He gave another of those shrugs and said, "As usual. They believed medicine was being administered. It is necessary to keep them so from becoming politically active again."

"Okay," I said. "Now give me a rundown on the clientele and the distribution."

He didn't bother to analyze my question. Instead, he simply rattled off names that didn't mean anything to me until he included Victor Sable, told me that distribution was taken care of by the guards, the payoff going to the ranking officers, with the biggest cut reserved for Russo Sabin. Payment would be made on delivery of the shipment, with collections going through Russo's office well screened by a lot of paperwork. No questions would be asked and for agenting the deal Fucilla got 5 percent of my end.

I took my time before I said, "The cut's steep enough. It's easy to see why you have a shortage of the stuff here. Not many other guys would want to buy in on the deal."

His little eyes glinted at me. "Not unless they have a rather unusual source of supply." His fingers stroked the cigar and spun it around between his lips again. "Perhaps you do."

"I wouldn't be a bit surprised."

"Ah, then we can do business," he said pleasantly.

"Maybe."

"There is something else?"

I nodded. "I don't like setting myself up for a target. If there's money behind those guys in the Castle and one of them kicks off, there's enough money to buy me a casket. Hot-tempered Latin types with close family ties hold a grudge a long time. They could buy my name and get me picked off and that I don't like."

Fucilla frowned, watching me closely. "So?"

"So I want to see those clients personally. Healthy addicts I can supply. If they're ready to kick off, forget it."

"I can assure you . . ." he bristled.

"Balls," I said. "I see it for myself or it's no deal. I can make out someplace else. It happens that I'm here and I can clear a nice profit, but I want to live to spend it. Dodging some contract killer those families could hire isn't up my alley."

Fucilla thought it over a moment, then bobbed his head. "In that case, we would demand assurances too."

"Like what?"

"Your ability to deliver and the quality of your merchandise."

"Fine," I told him. "You'll get a sample to analyze with a full shipment available immediately after I see who's getting it." I paused, then: "Now, do I import openly or use my own methods?"

His smile had a little humor in it. "I suggest, señor, that

you adopt your own ways. Our present government must put on a front, so to speak; therefore they are against the traffic in narcotics and will not hesitate to confiscate what they find for the sake of publicity. However, I can mention that they are most lenient in their approach to prevention of such events."

"I take my chances, is that it?"

His shrug was eloquent. "We all take our chances, señor." Then he added brightly, "But we are all alive, no?"

"For now," I said.

"Very well. When shall we . . . how do you say it? Get together?"

"I'll need two days."

"And the contact point?"

"The bar at the Regis Hotel."

He nodded, then let his eyes drift toward Rosa Lee. "Promptly at six. I go on duty an hour later. And her?"

"I'll pay her a finder's fee myself. She's not on percentage."

"Ah, very good," He got up, his official arrogance back once again, bowed curtly to Rosa and shook my hand with a quick limp motion. "It has been a pleasure, señor."

Rosa darkened the house again, let Fucilla out and stood at the window watching him disappear into the night. Without turning around she said, "You are doing a dangerous thing, Señor Morgan. They will be expecting a delivery."

"They'll get it."

She turned slowly and her face was a pale oval in the gloom. "Morgan . . ." This time her tone had changed and I knew why.

I said, "Only the sample, Rosa. It's my way into the Castle. Like you said . . . the smell of money. They'll do anything for it."

"And by this means, you will be able to extricate Victor Sable from the prison?"

"I hope so."

"Can I be of further help?"

"Yes. Contact Art Keefer and tell him his friend needs a pat on the back."

"But . . ."

"He'll understand. It means two ounces of pure heroin. We called it that when we used it for currency in some strange places in the old days."

I saw the outline of her smile. "You are a very odd person, Señor Morgan." She walked up to me and I could smell the wild, flowery perfume that was like a part of her. Very gently she placed both hands on my chest. "Someday I would like to know you much better."

"Maybe . . ." Then I stopped because her hands moved quickly and did something so unexpected it stopped the words in my throat. Her face blurred as it tilted up to me, the gentle movement of her fingers a jarring sensation. It wasn't a kiss, just a momentary dart of her tongue before I could move, then she stepped back.

"Yes, we Latin types are very hot-blooded and it has been much too long for me. Much too long." She held out her hand and I took it without realizing it. "Another time, Morgan. Now you must leave. There is much to be done."

8

THE NIGHT HAD a funny feeling to it. Maybe it was the hurricane that was being birthed somewhere in the moist air of the Caribbean, but the oppressive finger of danger was still there, reaching out to touch something. Trees that were normally still cast shadows against the greater darkness, their movements suggestive and capable of concealing any other slight motions.

I picked my way and time as carefully as I could, skirting lights and other people until I had covered a mile, picked up a cab that took me within a few blocks of the hotel, then retraced my course into the hotel.

Kim answered my knock and I stepped inside, expecting those big dark eyes to wipe me out with one suspicious glance. But they didn't. They had a funny, twinkly look of don't-give-a-damn resignation, and when I saw the empty magnum of champagne I knew why.

"Have a happy night?" I grinned.

She took a deep breath and almost burst through the lapels of the royal-blue housecoat that made an hourglass of her magnificent figure. "I have been simply drowning the speculative thoughts of what I would say if you had showed up dead or not at all."

"You have a receipt for my body," I laughed at her.

"A live body," she reminded me. "Besides, the department takes a dim view of an uncompleted mission."

"And I'm not to be trusted," I said.

"Naturally. Why should you? That's why I have the dubious pleasure of this assignment."

"So give up on me."

"I can't. You're the X factor. The unknown quantity. I can't stand to see a problem unsolved." She picked up a half-full glass and wrinkled her nose at the little bubbles that atomized at the surface of its pale contents. "Possibly because I was a psychology major at the university."

I brushed past her and uncorked the other bottle, filled a glass and downed the wine.

Kim said softly, "You smell funny."

"What?"

"You were with a girl."

"Knock it off." I filled the glass again and turned around. Her eyes weren't twinkling anymore. The cold was back and something more.

"I made a mistake. It isn't the X factor at all."

"Oh?"

"The delta factor," she said.

"It's all Greek to me," I told her.

There was something in her expression I couldn't quite read. "Delta," she repeated, "the phallic symbol for a woman. The triangle. The personal little geometric design that identifies the female from the male. The eternal triangle." She looked at me long and hard. "You and your damn broads."

Slowly, the implication came to me. "Quit blowing smoke," I said. "It's all part of the job. Besides, what the hell do you care?"

The eyes changed, but again, I couldn't read their meaning. "I don't, really," Kim said. She sipped at her glass, watching me over its rim. "I'd like a report."

So I gave it to her. She listened, committing it to memory, then said, "That's all?"

I had to grin again. "That's all I'm going to tell you. The delta factor is my own business."

"Not if it interferes with the project."

"Then maybe marriage should have its own responsibilities."

Her eyes glared at me this time. "Go screw yourself, Morgan."

"It isn't physically possible," I said and finished the champagne. "Anything new around here?"

Those eyes ran up and down me before they cooled off, then she set the glass down and curled herself into a chair, folding the housecoat over her legs with an unconscious gesture. "I had an agency contact."

I felt myself stiffen. "You nuts? We're supposed to be solo. . . ."

"Don't be so naïve, Morgan. It was prearranged in case of an emergency with a selected code so the conversation couldn't be understood."

"There wasn't any emergency," I said. I felt like belting her right in the mouth.

"There was an exigency, then."

I waited.

"The exploits of you and your wartime associates set a pattern for that forty-million-dollar robbery. I wanted a check on the one you called Sal Dekker."

"So you're back to that again. Did you get it?"

"With no trouble. Your old buddy is dead. He was killed in an automobile accident in Sydney, Australia, over a year ago and his body shipped back to his parents, who had it buried in their family plot with military honors."

"And what's all that supposed to indicate?"

"It throws the whole affair right back in your lap, doesn't it, Morgan?"

"Go screw yourself," I said.

"It isn't physically possible," she told me flatly.

My tone was just as flat. "Too bad," I said. "Why the sudden renewed interest? I was tried and sentenced. They can't add to it."

"Serving the sentence doesn't give you proprietary rights to Federal money. This mission completed reduces your jail term; restitution of the funds might help some more."

I let her see all my teeth in a great big grin. "Horse manure, lovely doll. Any aces I have up my sleeve I keep there or play out to take the pot. You never did get to know me very well."

"Nor do I intend to."

"Maybe now it's time for the rape job."

The little gun was in her hand without any noticeable movement. "Don't try it, Morgan."

"Someday I'm going to take that away from you and you know what I'm going to do with it?"

"Tell me, Morgan."

I let out a low laugh. "Nah," I said, "I don't think that's physically possible either." Instead of the expected cold flooding her eyes again, there was that little twinkle and I said, "Get dressed. I'd like to make an appearance downstairs."

"Wouldn't that be strange for a honeymooning couple?"

"There's been time enough to do what we were going to do. They'll think it's a ten-minute break."

"Male pride," she said scornfully.

"Masculine surety, kid," I told her. "On me it sticks out all over."

The gaming rooms of the hotel casino weren't as crowded as usual. Conversation seemed to be smothered by an unseen haze and the play at the tables was almost lackadaisical. Winning streaks generated only a polite show of interest and more people were at the several bars than had been previously. A crowd was grouped around the desk checking out, another making airline reservations back to the mainland and when I asked a bellboy about the situation he merely shrugged and said the weather had something to do with it.

Angelo was a little more specific. He indicated some of the maintenance crew lugging four-by-eight sections of half-inch plywood to the front of the building and told me that the weather advisory reports positioned the hurricane five hundred miles out and moving toward the island faster than expected. There was a possibility of it swinging northwest, but a lot of the guests weren't taking any chances. They were leaving while there was still time.

You could smell it even inside. It was all there. Everything piling up at once. That moving finger was preselecting its targets, lining them up, then withdrawing to deliver the full impact of a lethal punch.

I split with Kim, leaving her to play out a streak at the roulette wheel while I roamed between the aisles looking for the action. I stopped at the crap table, the only place that had a crowd and edged myself in when a player left in disgust. I threw a brace of chips on the field numbers and the dark-haired guy with the lopsided grin who was rolling the dice looked up at me with a challenging glance, spun the dice out, then grimaced when I picked up my winnings. Everybody but me was playing the lines so he simply smiled, said, "Lucky," and tossed the cubes out again. This time he made his point.

The next two rolls I lost on the field, made part of it back while the shooter was still trying for his six, then held back while he made it and raked in his chips.

He looked up with another of those crooked grins and said, "You ought to play on my side, feller."

"I'm a lousy gambler," I told him.

"Not from what I seen," he laughed. "I was there when you stopped the table the last time, remember?" He picked up the dice, shook them and threw his roll with a practiced toss and came up a three. The next pass he sevened out and said, "Well, you can't win 'em all," and crinkled his face in a laugh that threw his features out of shape. "Easy come, easy go. You going to roll 'em tonight?"

I shook my head. "I know when I've had it," I told him. I stepped back and let the sequin-gowned fat dame beside me take the dice.

"It's the weather," the guy told me and stuck out his hand. "Marty Steele, in case you forgot."

"From Yonkers," I answered, remembering him.

He offered me a cigarette and when I turned it down stuck one in his mouth and lit it. "You cutting out with the rest?"

"I don't know. It's a hell of a way to wreck a honeymoon."

"Yeah. I saw your bride. Quite a woman, that one. You sure got the luck. Me, I always wind up with some twist who cleans me out and takes off." He shrugged and grinned again. "Maybe I'm better off at that."

He tried to keep his tone light, but there was a reserved growl behind it and the remnants of the grin had lost its humor to an expression of near hate that lasted a split second before it came under control. Whatever bugged this guy was going to explode someday if he couldn't keep a lid on himself. He yanked the cigarette from his mouth with a peculiar arm motion, grimaced, then looked at me again. "Guess this damn storm coming in got everybody edgy."

"The planes are still leaving," I suggested.

"I'm not that edgy. Let the tourists blow. The big money boys are sticking it out and I plan to make a little loot at the tables. I waited a long time to see some of this action I've been hearing about and no damn storm is going to blow it on me."

"Well," I said, "hope you make out."

"Yeah, sure."

I walked off toward the roulette wheel where Kim was losing her chips one at a time, saw her frown of annoyance when she missed by one number and the grim determination of the amateur gambler when she placed another chip on the same digit.

With the crowd thinned out the security personnel were even more noticeable. The tension had touched them too and they stood in small groups eyeing the guests nervously. The sight of money leaving Nuevo Cádiz was going to leave a lot of tempers short.

I angled over toward the bar, ordered a cold beer and had it halfway down when I spotted Lisa Gordot down at the other end. She sat on a stool against the wall, her fingers curled around the glass so tightly her knuckles showed white and every few seconds her shoulders would tighten with some pent-up emotion. She raised her head a moment and I saw her eyes, filmed and red-rimmed from crying.

Carrying the beer, I walked around the bunch at the bar and came up behind her. "Why the gloom, kitten?"

There was no warmth in her smile; despair had wiped it out. "Morgan," she said hoarsely, "I'd appreciate it if you left me alone."

"You were happy when I left you, girl. What's got you down?"

"Nothing."

"I thought you'd be leaving." I finished the beer and slid the glass on the bar top. "You could lose yourself in the rush."

She answered with a dismal shake of her head. "No use, Morgan. My fat little protector thought of everything."

"Russo Sabin?"

"My protector," she nodded slowly. "He has my passport."

"Money can buy another one. Hell, you can get political asylum in some other country."

"You touched the sensitive nerve, Morgan. Money. He knew about my winnings. He had it confiscated under a dubious pretext of me being held at the request of another government until my legal status has been cleared. I'm a damn prisoner in this stinking hellhole."

"Suppose you had a ticket out?"

She picked up her glass, studied it a moment and drained the drink without pause. When she put the glass down she shook her head again. "What good would that do? You think his men aren't at the airport? They have their orders."

"There's got to be some way."

"I'm afraid not, Morgan. Not until Sabin is finished with me. It isn't a very pleasant thought at all. I have heard of others who came under his . . . paternal protection."

"But if there is a way? Would you take it?"

A glimmer of hope came into her eyes, faded, then brightened again. "Is there?"

"Let me think it out."

Her hand came out and lay on top of mine. "Why, Morgan?"

"Because I'd like to see that fat little bastard take a fall."

"Not just for me then?"

"For you too."

"I pay back my debts, Morgan."

"No payment expected, Lisa."

"I'll insist on it. I can be very persistent. There are things I know that come only to the most fortunate of women and . . ."

I grinned at her. "Don't tempt me. Go to your room and stay there until I contact you. If I call I'll ring once, hang up, wait a minute, then ring again. Make it look like you're sulking. At least Sabin will understand that. Meanwhile with this hurricane playing around and all the suckers evacuating, there will be plenty to keep him busy."

"Morgan . . ." She breathed in so that the swell of her breasts firmed the folds of her dress suggestively. "Thank you. Even if you can't . . . arrange things I'll still be grateful. Anytime."

The management had posted a hurricane tracking chart on the wall beside the desk, positioning the site of the storm, but optimistically had indicated probable course changes that might follow the path of previous blows that bypassed the island, each of the others traced in various colored lines. There were positive assurances that there was no immediate danger, that buildings were hurricane-proof and storm shelters were available and well stocked. All flights were on schedule if there was any trepidation on the part of the guests, with the airlines confirming extra flights if there was any danger whatsoever.

Maybe nobody but me noticed, but somebody had taken down the ornate brass-bound barometer that formerly occupied the place where the chart was. When I finished reading the report I went to turn around and a chill voice said, "Leaving, Señor Morgan?"

"Ah, Major Turez," I said. It was the first time I had seen him since he and Carlos Ortega paid us a visit. "No, I've weathered out hurricanes before."

His tight smile meant nothing. "That simplifies matters, señor. Perhaps you have a few minutes?"

"As a matter of fact, I don't." Then I saw the other two moving in at a minute nod of his head. "Maybe I do at that," I told him.

"Good." He waved his hand to one side. "This way please."

Carlos Ortega was behind the desk, Russo Sabin beside him and four uniformed soldiers stationed impassively beside the two doors of the office. A blue haze of acid cigar smoke hung in the air like smog, coming from the thin black twists in the pair at the desk.

An empty chair was placed in the middle of the room, and the major, looking crisp and efficient, nodded toward it. "Please be seated, Mr. Morgan."

I wasn't going to let these slobs fake me out. I didn't know what the hell they wanted and didn't much care, so I slouched in the chair and swung one leg over the other. Before they could ask I said, "What's the pitch? I'm getting a little fed up with all the attention."

Ortega looked at me, amused, like a wild, vicious cat playing with a moth. There was little subtlety in the man. There was that inborn savageness in him that made him enjoy any excuse to bring it out and now he was liking what he was doing. But I knew what he was after and knew he'd have to stay cool if he expected to get it.

"There is no reason to be defensive, Señor Morgan," he said. "No accusation has been made against you."

"Why should there be?"

He turned to face Russo Sabin. "It is that our Director of Police would like to ask you some questions."

"Go ahead."

I was a little too calm and flippant to satisfy Sabin. His eyes half closed in his fat face and his little mouth pursed in an unspoken obscenity. Then he said, "You can account for your whereabouts tonight?"

"Sure. If you can't you got a bunch of nitheads watching me."

"That doesn't answer the question."

I made a disgusted gesture. "I was in my room enjoying my honeymoon."

Sabin nodded ponderously, then laced his fingers together and asked smugly, "You can prove this, of course?"

This time I gave him a look of contempt. "Yeah, I had six witnesses watching me consummate my marriage."

One of the uniformed guards snickered and Ortega withered him with a glance. When he turned back to me his face was rock hard. "This is not a time to make jokes, señor."

"So who's joking? The bellboy brought us up supper and champagne, my wife and I had a ball for a few hours, then we came downstairs and dropped some money in the casino."

"Isn't that unusual for a honeymooning couple?" Sabin asked.

"There are times when too much can be enough," I told him. "Anybody who ever had a woman knows that."

I watched his face get red and his fingers squeeze together. "What's this about?" I said.

Sabin didn't answer me. Instead, he stated, "Earlier you and your wife visited a certain restaurant. There you had supper, spent money lavishly and foolishly and entertained a dancer at your table."

"Anything wrong with that?"

There was a pause of several seconds, then Sabin bobbed his head again. "Inasmuch as that young lady was found dead a short time ago, yes."

It was back again, that strange smell of danger. But the peculiar part was, it didn't come from the faces I was looking at.

Sabin said, "Perhaps you'd like to repeat your conversation."

"Hell, I was half gassed. My wife chewed me out for even speaking to the broad. Outside of a few compliments I don't remember what I said." I shifted in the chair. "You had your men tailing me. Didn't they tell you what went on?"

"To a point. Your conversation wasn't audible."

"Tough," I told him. "What happened to the broad?"

"Strangled, señor. A most heinous crime."

I played it as straight as I could. "Well damn right it is, but I don't see where I come into it."

Sabin's face shaped itself into another self-satisfied expression. All of them were watching me now, waiting for any indication that I was lying. "Supposing I tell you that you were seen leaving the hotel at a specified time from an exit normally unknown to guests? Supposing I tell you that you were followed to a taxicab whose number was taken down and whose driver later identified you as a fare he drove to a street not far from the murdered woman's?"

But I had been through too many interrogations before. I let out a short laugh and looked square into those pig eyes. "Supposing you do, buddy. What am I supposed to say? Whatever happened to the tails you had on me? Who saw all this? And if I set out to see a broad just to knock her off, you think I'd let some taxi driver identify me? Come off it, I'm not that stupid. You try pulling a frame on me to get your hands on forty big fat millions that still belong to the United States Government and I'll blow a whistle so loud the Navy will park a battleship in your backyard."

Very softly, Ortega said, "That wouldn't do *you* much good, Señor Morgan."

I got up then and stood there, playing the hand right out to the end. "Maybe not, feller, but you'd get your noses wiped in your own crap. Don't give me any of your garbage because I won't take it. I told you once before, this isn't amateur night in the bingo parlor."

It was my attitude that did it. I caught the quick scowl that clouded Ortega's face, then the sudden look of consternation that touched Sabin's eyes. I said, "Where did you pick up all this junk?"

Sabin was caught off balance and said, "There was a phone call."

I pushed it just a bit further. "Anonymous, no doubt." I saw his tongue flick out around his lips and knew I had it. "Big deal, Director of Police. I made a lot of enemies in my time, so now somebody spots me and makes a call. Maybe that one was tailing me too, so he bumps a broad and drops it in my lap and you're idiot enough to go for it. You could use some training in police technique."

Sabin's face went red with suppressed rage. "There was the taxi driver, Señor Morgan . . ."

"Nuts to that too. When does a cabdriver examine his fares at night? Get him here and let him try to make a positive i.d. on me." I gave him another disgusted look and deliberately spit on the floor. "You guys are wasting your time." Then I pulled the clincher. "Or is it because I happened to get a little friendly with your girl friend, Director? Lisa Gordot seems to be a woman who can use a friend."

Russo Sabin seemed to shrink inside himself. He half turned toward Carlos Ortega and saw those eyes watching him blankly with deliberately concealed malice because they thought he was exposing an entire organization through sheer stupidity over a woman.

Casually, Ortega said, "I think that will be all, Señor Sabin."

The Director of Police was glad to get out of there, but not before he challenged me with one glance of pure hatred that meant it was only the beginning. With a wave of his hand Ortega motioned for the guards and Major Turez to follow him, then he leaned on the desk, his shoulders hunched like an animal anticipating a fight.

"You could be a clever liar, Morgan."

"Why bother?"

"*That's* what bothers me. A man in your situation is in

no position to change the *status quo*. Here you have sanctuary of a sort. Why should you jeopardize it? You have touched Señor Sabin in a sore spot. I have known about the Gordot woman some time now. However, he is a reliable man whose judgment I never before had to question. It seems unlikely that it should be done so now."

"He wouldn't be the first guy to tumble over a woman," I said. "But if it helps matters any, tell him I'm not interested in his broad so keep the heat off me."

"He will be informed." He leaned back in his chair and puffed at the cigar, oblivious to the foul smell. "Now, there is another matter."

"Oh?"

"The matter of forty million dollars you mentioned."

"I see."

"Naturally, that is too much for you ever to spend even at discounted rates."

"Naturally."

"It is a shame not to see so much fine currency in circulation, especially where it could be useful to a cause."

"Naturally," I repeated.

"There are ways for it to be distributed so that everyone could profit with little risk." He shrugged to emphasize his point. "Of course, this country is autonomous and one can be safe within its confines."

"As long as it pleases you," I reminded him.

"Quite right, Señor Morgan," he said. "And there are forty million ways of pleasing me." The smile left his face and all that raw power came back. "Then, too, incurring my displeasure means nothing to me, but a great deal to you."

"I'll think about it."

"Do not take too long. To expedite your thinking I have already informed your government that you are within our jurisdiction. We have no extradition agreement with the United States so we are quite capable of either returning you to your country or seeing that you have an unfortunate accident. I am really not impressed with having a battleship parked in my front yard. There would be that eventuality only if they could be sure of having you alive and their money intact with the possibility that they might extract its location from you."

"Clever," I said.

"Yes. I think so. I would not take too long to think it over, Morgan. Nor would I try leaving if I were you."

"Hell, I like it here. Everybody's so damn friendly." I

turned around and walked to the door, stopping with it half open. "How long do I have to think about it?" I asked him.

"While it is still your choice," he told me.

I nodded, knowing what he was thinking. What he didn't realize was that I knew that someplace in Miami he had a man ready to get into that safe-deposit box they had set up for me and when it happened the guy would be nailed cold. It wouldn't take Ortega too long to figure the deal out and when he did the trap would shut on me, but in the meantime I could stretch things out a little longer.

When I stepped outside and closed the door I started toward the roulette wheel. As I passed the crap table a figure leaned back from the players and Marty Steele said, "You keep lousy company, Winters." He pointed his head to where Sabin and the others were talking at the desk. While I watched them they finished their conversation and walked to the main doors.

"Don't I though?"

"Those clowns are rough. If you're on the con, cut out, friend. They're worse than the cops in Vegas. They even bugged me some because I came in alone and traveling light and stayed longer than the usual tourist."

"They didn't want anything from me," I said.

His face went into another one of those lopsided smiles that looked like his jaw was out of joint. "Just passing the word. They don't even like big winners."

"The hell with them."

"Me too," he said, and turned back to the game.

I spotted Kim at the wheel and this time she had a three-inch stack of chips in front of her. She got the message I flashed to her with my eyes, cashed in her chips and followed me out.

We couldn't take any chances on the room having been bugged again during our absence, so we made small talk, noises like a loving couple, then went into the bathroom and turned the shower on full blast while she perched on the edge of the tub and I sat on the lip of the john and explained it to her. I was talking more to myself than to Kim, using her for a sounding board, and she knew it, not interrupting, but letting me get it out of my system.

"They got a call, all right. That's what made Sabin so mad. He can't figure the angle himself. Nobody knew I was leaving here except Angelo and you and I can't see him in that picture. That leaves it up to pure coincidence and even that doesn't smell right. I didn't bust out fast. I made damn sure I was clear before I went to Rosa Lee's place. If I was spotted, then it was because somebody was pretty suspicious of my exit and was good enough to follow me without being seen and that isn't likely of anybody who just happened to be there. That leaves only two other alternatives . . . that I was seen leaving or somebody was waiting for a move like that. Neither one makes sense. I know I didn't have a tail on me going out of here and who the hell would be waiting for me to go out like I did?"

"Could somebody have been watching Rosa's place?" Kim suggested.

"Then how would they get the cab number? No, I was tailed, all right. Somebody followed me as far as Rosa's and killed her. Putting it on me was only a cover."

"Sabin didn't mention you being followed back."

"No, and that's a point I want to square away. Go out and call Angelo. Tell him to bring up some more champagne."

She got on the phone and five minutes later Angelo was in the room with another iced bucket of champagne. When I called him into the bathroom he looked at me oddly, then I asked, "How do you stand with Ortega's crowd, Angelo?"

"Why not ask me what you intend to ask me, señor?"

Sometimes you have to take a chance. I threw it at him. "A girl named Rosa Lee was killed not long ago."

His eyes never left mine. "Yes, I know. You were accused."

"How do you know?"

"Carlos Ortega is not the only one with mechanical ears, señor."

"Any explanation?"

He shook his head. "At the moment, none. When we find that one, it will be over very slowly for him."

"You think it was me?"

"I do not think so, señor. Others, they are not so sure. They have asked me the same thing."

"And . . . ?"

"I told them the same thing."

"Can you check something out for me?"

"I will be most pleased."

"There's a man named Juan Fucilla, a guard at the Rose Castle. I want to find out where he is."

"Could he be the one?"

"I doubt it."

"May I ask why you inquire about this one?"

"To see if he's still alive."

"Then I can assure you that he is. Before I came up I saw Señor Fucilla on the patio having a drink with one of our more notorious prostitutes. He frequents this establishment often. The woman is one of his favorite companions."

"Okay, Angelo, thanks." I didn't bother to explain any further and he didn't ask any questions.

After he had left, Kim said, "What was all that?"

I went out, grabbed the bottle and tumbler, then went back to the bathroom. I popped open the champagne and spilled some of it into a glass. "Whoever followed me there didn't hang around to see Fucilla come in. He knew the direction I had to take back, waited until I had passed him and went back and killed Rosa."

"Why?"

"I wish I knew, kid," I said.

"She was engaged in antigovernment activities."

"No, it wasn't Ortega's people. They wouldn't have killed her outright. They would have held her and tried to squeeze the names of the others out of her. This was something else. It ties in with the shot somebody took at us."

Kim's brow knitted in a frown and she tossed her hair back with a gesture of annoyance. "Perhaps not. If somebody *had* wanted to kill you, he would have had the chance at Rosa's house."

"And maybe he didn't want to expose himself when there was a better way out. In that case Rosa meant nothing to him except a girl I was with for a while."

"But *who?*" Kim insisted.

"Somebody's been keeping an eye on me. It's only a feeling I have, but it's the only one that makes sense."

"You think they might know why we're here?"

I waited a minute, then said, "No, it isn't that at all. At least I hope not. If Rosa made the contact with Art Keefer before she was killed we still might keep this machine in motion. She was the only source of communication with the mainland I have. If it was a simple kill then Sabin wouldn't have any reason to tear her place apart and come up with the radio transmitter. If politics were involved, then we're in a spot."

"I still have my contact left."

"You're looking to get us both killed. I was supposed to make the arrangements in and out, remember? All we need is for the Soviets to know we're taking an extralegal hand in political affairs here and that gives them the right to step in too. With Cuba on the Red side, this area would make a neat little secondary base to plant their operation in."

"Just the same, we'd better move fast."

"I intend to," I told her. "Where's your passport?"

She gave me a strange look, then reached in her handbag and passed it to me. The name and picture were going to have to be changed and the impressed seal faked, but that shouldn't be any trouble. I went to the corner of the room, lifted the rug from the matting under it and raked out some of the larger-denomination bills I had stashed there. I took five thousand from the pile, stacked the others into a small sheaf and threw them on the table. "Take care of that," I said.

Kim watched me carefully, wondering what I was up to. When I pulled my coat on she asked, "Where to now?"

"Favor to a friend. I'm getting Lisa Gordot out of this place."

Her eyes flashed fire at me, her body tense with anger. "If you think . . ."

"Can it, sugar. I want Russo Sabin off balance as far as I can get him. The more trouble they have the quicker they'll tip their hand."

Only the discipline she had learned at the academy kept her from throwing something at me. I gave her a pleasant little grin, blew a kiss at her and left.

Angelo was glad to do me a service. He photographed Lisa with a Minox camera right in her room, promised a serviceable passport within the next few hours, then left after cautioning me that Señor Sabin had positioned guards at strategic points around the hotel with specific orders to detain either Lisa, Kim or me if any of us attempted to make a break for it.

The look of hope Lisa had evaporated slowly as she sat in the big chair facing me. She had changed into a gown of some shimmering silver material that clung to her with skinlike tenacity, but inside it the vibrant quality of the woman had wilted into the static effect of a mannequin.

Her eyes, dry now, had no luster to them. "There really isn't much use to try now, is there?"

I plucked the roll of bills from my pocket and handed them to her. "Don't quit so easily. Busting out of this place won't be that hard and shaking Sabin's men can be arranged. You'll make a plane out of here if you don't run scared and do what I tell you to. Hell, you're not dead yet."

She let me see the tiniest of smiles. "Yes . . . that's quite true."

"And this isn't the first jam you've been in."

This time her laugh was real. "More true than ever. I wish you'd tell me why you're doing all this."

"You're my diversion, Lisa. You're going to help split their forces. History records a lot of governments that fell because of a woman."

"And what do you get out of it, Morgan?"

"If you're real curious, look me up in some back issue of any newspaper when you have time. It won't be nice, but it will be interesting. I'm really typecast. Probably the only character who can pull this stunt off."

"Morgan . . ." She came out of the chair, the dress making a soft, slithering sound. "Whether you do or not, I'm still appreciative." Her arms went around my neck and with a provocative motion of her tongue she wet her lips and touched them to my mouth. There was nothing static about her now. Under my hands she quivered and when I kneaded my fingers in the smooth flesh of her shoulders she moaned softly into the kiss, felt for my hand and pressed it against the hard rise of her breast, her body curving forward to flow against my own.

I pushed her away and held her face in my hands. "No, kid."

Her eyes fought me. "Why?"

"Because we need the tension. We have to stay tight. Relax and it's dead time."

"You're a bastard, Morgan." But she smiled, knowing what I meant. "I won't let you get away, you know."

I nodded. "I know. Someday . . . another time, another place."

"But someday soon," she added.

I shut and locked the door behind me and walked into the suite. The wall radio that had been playing a fast flamenco number suddenly was interrupted to give another optimistic weather report from the local government station, stressing the lack of necessity for anyone making a hurried departure.

She was so nearly motionless that I didn't notice her at first, sitting at the end of the couch in the shadows. There was something odd about the way she watched me pour a drink, only her eyes following my movements. On top of the glass-covered table in front of her were three five-hundred-dollar bills.

I walked over and stood looking down at her. "What's bugging you? I wasn't gone long enough to go the delta-factor route."

Kim's eyes never left mine. "We're back to the X factor again, Morgan." Her voice was completely frosted. "Look at those bills."

I frowned, put the glass down and inspected the money. Good solid U.S. currency. "What about them?"

"They're part of what you left here. Where did you get them?"

"Now how the hell would I know?" I tossed them back, irritated at her manner. "They either came from the bank in Miami or the tables downstairs."

"You had some of your own funds too, didn't you?"

"A little. Why?"

"Was it a little, Morgan, or a whole lot? Maybe a whole bundle you could pass over here without being detected?"

"What are you talking about?"

"The serial numbers on those bills match those in that forty-million-dollar robbery you staged."

"Look . . ." I started.

She shook her head, her expression cold and accusing. "And I was just beginning to think . . ." She stood up, stared at me hard and added, "Never mind."

9

AND NOW THE LITTLE things were starting to fall into place. The probables were balancing out against the possibles and a fine thread was drawing them together. They still made a wavy, indiscernible line, but as the threat tightened the line would straighten and the pattern would become visible.

Time was all it took, and that was running out fast.

I let the day go past, ignoring the occasional contemptuous glances Kim threw my way. Twice I went down to the casino, noticing that the crowd had diminished by half, with more leaving every hour. The hurricane tracking chart showed that the storm, which had swung northward for three hours, had veered back into its original course and was approaching Nuevo Cádiz with unhurried deliberation, picking up in intensity as it moved. There was still a good possibility of it cutting out again erratically, but not too many seemed willing to take the chance.

The huge plate-glass windows of the casino that fronted on the street had been taped and boarded over, but through the still open main doors I could see the activity on the street, the lines of taxis going to the airport, the overloaded wagons piled with household goods and wide-eyed kids coming into the city for greater protection against the storm.

Outwardly it was just another beautiful tropical day, the sun warm and red in a bright blue sky, with only a few wisps of high-altitude clouds in the southeast. Yet there was an oppressive sensation about it all. A dozen birds wheeled overhead, their senses alerted to the thing bearing down on them, calling to each other with shrill, annoyed screeches.

For a half hour I watched the unconcerned play at the tables and even tried a couple of spins of the roulette wheel, but it wasn't a day for winners and the stickmen were encouraging any kind of activity they could. Whatever hung in the air was too stifling to interest the players and they stayed with the games only out of habit or instinct.

For me there was more than just that heavy feeling. There was that strange warm spot between my shoulder blades, the knowledge that it was an exposed target area and somebody was preselecting it. The past had held too many similar occasions for me to ignore it. It wasn't a premonition, simply a combination of circumstances only my subconscious recognized and flashed a danger signal to that one spot in my back.

I turned slowly, surveying the faces in the casino. Some of Ortega's people I knew by sight, some were so casual in their behavior as to be obvious. I spotted Marty Steele, who happened to look up while I was watching him, threw me a short wave and went back to the game. The regulars couldn't have cared less for the storm and played with no show of concern, but the tourists kept checking their watches and consulting the flight schedules every so often, marking time until they could take off.

But there was nobody I could lay a finger on. Just the same, that warm spot wouldn't go away. I was going to pick up a drink at the bar, then saw Angelo, caught his signal and moved to the elevator bank instead. At this time of day they were on automatic and when we stepped into an empty and pushed the floor button we were alone.

There wasn't much time, so Angelo gave it to me as quickly as he could. "The altered passport has been delivered to Señorita Gordot as you wished, señor. This evening she will receive a maid's uniform to wear over her clothes. Her ticket has been purchased in her name for Flight 51 tomorrow night. She will go out with the other maids when their shift is over and be driven to the airport in the truck of María López' brother."

"You sure of them?"

"As I am of my own mother, señor. They are of us as Rosa Lee was."

"Sabin has a watch on the airport, Angelo."

"I assume that as a woman she knows the art of makeup. It will not take too much imagination to make her look like a maid or a worried tourist in a hurry. I know those people there, señor. Customs is a big joke. It is Russo Sabin's own men we will have to be careful of, but that will be taken care of." He looked at me and smiled. "There are ways of attracting their attention elsewhere."

"Will they check on the tickets?"

"That is unlikely too. The airport people are not used to

such confusion. They will be glad to push them through as
fast as possible without asking questions. Once on board
the airliner she will be safe. The planes are taking off the
moment they are filled."

"You clear, kid?"

"I can take care of myself. You are the one who will be
in danger from Director Sabin."

"If that's all I have to worry about, I'll be happy," I
said. "What about tonight?"

"I will be free for one hour at exactly six o'clock. A call
at your room will be my last before I am relieved for my
supper."

"Good. I'll be waiting," I said as the elevator stopped
and he got off.

Kim wasn't in the room when I got there. Her handbag
was gone and so were the three five-hundred-dollar bills,
but the rest was back between the rug layers where I had
kept them. As far as I could tell, her clothes were all in
the closet. I scoured the room for a message, but she
hadn't left any.

I swore under my breath because she should have
known better. Nobody authorized her to do one thing on
her own except stay with me and if she were trying to
make anything out of those three bills that had turned out
she could be throwing a noose over both our necks.

The sun tucked itself under the horizon, leaving a pur-
plish glow before the night wiped it out and wrapped the
city in a moonless black mantle. Whatever had happened
to her, I couldn't go trying to track her down. At a few
minutes to six I slid the .45 into my waistband, made sure
I had the lock picks in my pocket and as I finished Angelo
knocked on the door.

He came in with the supper for two, pocketed the check
I signed that he would turn in later and said, "You are
ready, señor?"

"All set. What about the guard?"

"Satisfying his thirst with a bottle of wine in the house-
keeper's closet."

"And if they ask about it later?"

"He was the one to request it, señor. Shortly he will fall
asleep."

"Okay, let's go."

The route out was simplified by the lack of traffic in the
hotel. We made the basement through the service elevator,
sent the lift back to the main floor by hitting the button

before we hopped out, then picked our way past stacked cartons and barrels of dishes to a window that opened on an airshaft between the hotel and the building adjacent to it. Angelo forced open the window in the other building, squeezed down through it and motioned me to follow him. Once inside, I put my hand on his shoulder and let him lead me through a maze he seemed to be familiar with until we came to a service entrance that led to a side street.

Angelo wasn't taking any chances with cabs. A battered panel truck was parked at the curb and when Angelo motioned to it I jumped in and let him drive a circuitous route toward the house of Rosa Lee to make sure we weren't being followed.

We entered Rosa's house from the rear, the lock giving easily to the pick. I snapped the small flash on and let the beam probe the darkness. From what Angelo had found out, the police investigation had been limited to ascertaining the means and time of death and removal of the body. The prime suspect had been me, so other avenues of investigation had been dropped for the time being. At the moment Sabin's men were making inquiries among the many admirers Rosa had at the Orino Bar, following up the possibility that it might have been a crime of passion.

Angelo pointed to the kitchen. "She was killed there, señor."

I threw the beam around the room. Pieces of broken dishes were still scattered on the floor, a bread bin was overturned in the corner and its contents strewn all over the place and one of the two wooden chairs was flattened as if something had crashed on top of it.

"She put up a fight," I said.

"*Si*. She was much bruised."

I knelt down and raked pieces of the dishes into a pile and sorted them out. In three minutes I had them assembled enough to see what had been broken. One dinner plate, one cup, one saucer.

As Angelo watched the process curiously, I said, "She wasn't entertaining. Whoever did it came in the way we did and killed her as she was getting something to eat."

"I don't understand, señor."

"Never mind," I told him. "Come on."

He followed me out the back way to the old garage, watched while I jiggled open the padlock and came in through the door behind me. I let the light pick out familiar items, searching for any sign of disturbance, then ran it over the beam that concealed the radio transmitter.

Angelo said, "Señor . . ."

"No political angle, Angelo. She was killed because of me. Now listen carefully. If Sabin digs in hard enough he'll come up with either the right answer or some excuse to tear this place apart. There's a radio setup hidden back here your people can use. When I'm done with it, have it dismantled and taken to some safe place. Can you arrange it?"

"*Si*, with no trouble, señor."

"Good. Get somebody on it right away." I let him hold the light while I checked him out on the operation, then cut in the power, let the set warm up and dialed Art's frequency, hoping somebody was monitoring the channel. I gave the call signal five times before Art himself answered, made sure of my identity, then told me to go ahead.

I said, "Rosa's been killed, Art. Nothing on it yet and I haven't time to explain the details. Did she reach you?"

"Roger, Morgan. The stuff you requested is on the way. I blew a cylinder on the plane so it went out on the only boat available and you were damn lucky. Nothing's moving around here with the hurricane on the way. It will be landed at José's place and he'll get it up to you."

"Good . . ." I started to say.

"Hold it. You're getting some additional cargo besides. Your friend Joey Jolley made it down here and he's one hell of a scared boy. He wouldn't talk to me at all and insisted on seeing you so he hopped aboard the same boat too. The condition he's in I'd keep him under cover if I were you. I got the feeling he thought he was followed, and the guy who's taking the boat over told me at the last minute that somebody broke into his cabin. He had his course marked out on the chart in the pilothouse and I never gave that a thought because he said some booze was missing and it wasn't the first time it had happened."

"Joey mention any names?"

"Not to me he didn't."

"You sure no other boats are leaving?"

"Morg, after that last blow that ripped this place apart you couldn't get anything for hire for a million bucks. The guy coming in to you did it as a personal favor. I saved his neck for him twice. Your luck is still running if the storm doesn't hit."

"You kidding? How the hell are we supposed to get out of here? Can't you get that plane repaired?"

"Not a chance. No parts are available locally and it will be a week before they're delivered. All I can tell you is that you might be able to take the boat back if you can move that fast. If you don't get caught in the middle of the blow you might be able to outrun or outride it. It's a pretty seaworthy job with twin diesels and the captain knows his stuff."

"Will he stick around?" I asked him.

"I guarantee he'll wait until the last minute, but when he's ready to go he'll cut out and you'll be on your own. These guys aren't under orders these days, buddy, and he's got a wife and six kids to think of."

"Okay, Art, keep this channel open in case I need another contact."

"Will do. How's the project coming?"

"Change of plans. There isn't time for fancy footwork. It'll have to be a straight bust out."

"Think you can handle it alone?"

"Hell, man, who has a choice?"

I heard his low laugh before he signed off and I flipped the power switch. When I had the antenna down and the set back under wraps I made sure Angelo was familiar with its operation, then retraced my steps outside.

For a minute I stood in the darkness smelling the night, feeling the warm, humid air touch my skin. But the warm spot between my shoulders wasn't there anymore and I knew that whoever had been tracking behind me was waiting someplace else.

At five minutes past seven we parked the truck where we had found it and went back in the way we had come out. On my floor the guard was having a gentle sleep in a sitting position on a pile of packaged laundry, and Angelo waved me on so he could awaken him.

When I opened the door I knew she had come back. The suite was steamy from the open bathroom door and the scent of perfume seemed to dangle in the air. She came out of the bedroom in a fresh dark-blue silk suit, her hair glistening blackly in soft waves down around her shoulders. I went to the radio and turned it up nearly full volume in case there were listening ears.

All I could say was, "Where the hell have you been?"

Only for a second was there a slight trace of anger, then the cold professional attitude returned and she stalked past me to the sofa and sat down. "My contact called me."

"Damn it! How many times . . ."

She shut me up with a single look. "It was an emergency. Ortega got his man into Miami to hit the safe-deposit box we had set up. Our people closed in and got him. Unfortunately, there was an error in judgment. They didn't handcuff him and on the way out he made a break for it and got away. They think they have him holed up in a general area, but there may be the possibility that he can make contact with Ortega if they don't get to him in time."

I got it out of my system with a few choice words, then took a deep breath to cool off. "They had to be cute about it. Damn it, they had to be cute."

"What's done is done."

"Don't be so smug, sugar. It's your neck too."

"I knew the risk I was taking."

"So did I. That's why I feel like such a sap." I stopped and looked at her. "Where did you meet this contact?" I kept my voice at whisper level.

"Here in the hotel. He took a lower-level room like a lot of the other local businessmen are doing who have places along the beach. And don't worry about the guard. He never saw me go either way."

"How's this guy keep in touch with the mainland?"

"He has a radio unit built into a recorder he uses for business."

"Supposing the guy manages to reach Ortega?"

"Then we'll know about it too. The agency requested cooperation from the Naval Station at Key West to cover all frequencies in case of a transmission and relay the information to us. Since Ortega probably didn't expect this development they wouldn't have prepared a code, but in case they did the Navy will have their cryptographers ready."

"Okay. We'll just have to go along with it. Who is he and what room is he in?"

She hesitated a moment, then said, "Luis Rondo. Room 203. He's in the import-export business and has been a resident here eight years. Except for an initial police scrutiny by the police he has been accepted and runs a legitimate business at a profit. He has never been suspected of being planted here by our government. Two years ago he married a native who died a year later of cancer."

"Good enough."

"Now, what are your plans?" she asked me.

"First I want to clear Lisa Gordot out of here. That'll hit Sabin where it hurts and he'll split up his forces to try to scratch her out. The more we thin out that bunch the easier it'll be to operate."

"And if it doesn't work?"

"Let's try it first. We're playing this tune by ear all the way at this point. If anybody hits a wrong note it'll get lost in the shuffle."

With a touch of sourness she said, "That takes care of your delta business. Our primary target was Victor Sable. Or did you forget about him?"

"Stop the sarcasm," I said. "All we can do is wait." I filled her in on the latest details and let her absorb them. She wanted further information on Joey Jolley, but I told her it was none of her damn business and let it stand at that.

Kim wouldn't accept it that way. A wry smile twisted the corner of her mouth and she said, "You don't have to play any games for my benefit, Morgan. You've gone to some elaborate pains to make me think you were falsely accused and it isn't any use."

"What if it were true?"

She gave a meaningless shrug. "Why think of it?"

"You have a lot to learn, baby," I told her. "Now let's finish this honeymoon farce and get it over with. If things work right tomorrow's going to be a busy day." I walked over and turned the volume of the radio down so we could speak in normal tones again.

"Bedtime, doll?"

Her voice had a smile in it, but not her expression. "Wonderful idea," she said. She walked into the bedroom, threw a pillow and blanket at me and shut the door.

In the morning no one had to check the weather advisory to know where the hurricane lay. The sky was a dismal gray and a moist breeze blew in from the tip of the island, still too languid to dissipate the oppressive heat, but it was an early warning sign that the monster was building and heading steadily in our direction.

Bags were stacked beside the hotel desk with the guests busy demanding immediate space on outgoing flights. The same crowd was still at the table gambling, committed to staying and not giving a damn what happened.

Kim and I ate a silent breakfast in the Continental Room, a sallow-faced man with a bulge of a gun showing under his too tight suitcoat occupying the next table and trying to be inconspicuous behind a newspaper. When we finished Kim announced that she wanted to do some shopping and I told her to go ahead because I wanted to try the crap table again. I paid the bill and when we got up the tail decided to stay with her, figuring there were enough of the others in the casino to keep me under their eyes.

And that was the way I wanted it. As long as I was in sight they'd hold their places and let me move around. I made a point of having them spot me without the tail, pass the word around, then wandered aimlessly from table to table making a casual play here and there without winning.

Marty Steel was still trying to beat the faro game, his eyes red-rimmed from lack of sleep. He threw in his last few chips, lost, then reached in his pocket for a sheaf of bills and passed them to the dealer for another stack.

"Bad day?" I asked.

His head snapped around, startled at the intrusion, his face a strange mask before he recognized me and gave me that lopsided smile that seemed to send his jaw out of joint. " 'Bad' is no word for it, friend. I should have taken your advice and blown this coop. These guys are taking me broke."

`I nodded to the chips in front of him. "Better not tap your reserve."

"Don't worry, I'm still in good enough shape. You're going to ride it out, huh?"

"I'm sure not fighting that mob at the airport." I touched his shoulder. "See you later."

He said, "Right," and went back to his game.

Kim finished her shopping by two o'clock and joined me at the bar for a drink. Her tail had taken up a position at the other end, exhausted from following her on her tour. She had her arms full of packages and for the benefit of all the eyes we were nothing but a very loving couple. We held hands and kept our heads together, laughing a lot, but the talk was far from romantic.

I said, "Get up to the room and stay there until I join you. I want to set things up down here to look natural when I make my contact. When we break Lisa out we may need you for a decoy, so don't go running off."

"Have you thought what we'll do if you get Sable out and we don't make that boat?"

"Yeah, I'll cry a lot."

"Damn it, Morgan," she smiled maliciously, "will you remember we're dealing with national security?"

"How can I forget it with you to remind me? I love my

little parole officer, but she gets damn wearing after a while."

Her smile thinned out and she dug her nails into the back of my hand. "Maybe I should remind you of something else. I'm authorized to kill both you and Victor Sable rather than expose this project."

"You really that dedicated?"

Kim answered me with her eyes first, then answered truthfully, "Yes, I'm really that dedicated. And capable." She got up with another smile, gathered up her packages, patted my cheek and walked off. Her tail seemed to sigh to himself, then slid off his stool with regret and followed her to the elevators.

The trick to faking a drunk at a crowded bar was simply being a roving conversationalist, buying a lot of drinks, but leaving them standing untouched as you hopped around. If you ordered the same drink as the person you talked to and scooted off, he invariably drank it himself and not even the bartender got wise.

I took my time building the act, watching the hours roll by on my watch, getting a little louder and a lot friendlier with each drink, making a point of setting up anybody who joined the throng to a free round on me. Not even the waiters escaped my offers, though they declined politely. Twice cabdrivers came in looking for fares who had called for them and suddenly found a drink in their hands. I kept it at a level that wasn't obstreperous enough to be cut off, but enough to put the pair who were detailed to watch me at their ease, figuring a hard-spending tipsy customer was only an asset at that point.

When José came in I wasn't out of character in pulling him in next to me and calling loudly for a highball for my new buddy. When he had it in his hand I toasted him elaborately, making sure he was facing away from the watchers, and downed half my drink.

While my glass was still at my mouth I felt him slip something in my pocket and say, "There is a man with me, señor."

"I know. Where is he?"

"Outside in the car. What is to be done with this one? He insists on seeing you."

"Tell him to meet me right here and for Pete's sake make sure he comes in calm."

"He is a scared man, señor."

"So have him fake it."

"I will try."

"Then you get back to the boat and tell that captain to stand by as long as possible."

"With this hurricane approaching, I would not delay too long, señor. Already all the other boats are making for safe ports.

"Sure, José. Now beat it back and make that captain wait us out."

José's face studied me seriously. "I know whatever it is you do is for the good of our country, señor. I will do my best.

I cracked a couple of jokes he didn't get, but he caught the picture and went along with it and excused himself politely to walk away, a little man who could pass unseen in a crowd of two.

Fifteen minutes later Joey Jolley edged in the main doors, glanced around nervously until he located the bar and walked toward me like a man in a room full of tigers, his shoulders tense with fear that he repressed so hard a cold sweat glistened on his forehead.

I pulled the same act I did with José, but hissed between my teeth to make like I was a stranger and ordered a drink for him loud enough to carry down the bar. I kidded with him until nobody was paying any more attention when his drink came, but unlike José he didn't toy with his, but spilled it down in one fast gulp and set the glass back on the bar for a refill.

I said, "Easy, buddy, it's going to be a long night."

He didn't pay any attention. The second one went down the same way and he shuddered when it hit his stomach, his eyes misting a second before they cleared and rolled up to meet mine. "You know what you did to me, Morgan?" His voice was almost breathless. "It was Whitey Tass. He killed her, now he's . . ."

I kicked him square in the shins and he sucked in his breath as the pain of it cut him off short in midsentence. Marty Steele had seen me, edged in and slammed a bill on the bar with an order for a quick shot of Scotch. "Damn, what a miserable day this has been!" he blurted out. "You know I got hooked for six grand? I never saw cards go that long in one direction." He tossed his drink off and waited for another. "I'm calling it quits," he told me. He wrinkled his face in a grimace until the scar tissue around the bridge of his nose showed white, poured his drink down to follow the first one and waved the change off to the bartender. "See you tomorrow," he said, and left.

Joey was still holding his breath from the kick I had

given him and when I turned around grinning idiotically he said, "What was that for?"

"For being stupid. Quit mentioning names. Have one more drink, then walk off with me. I'm going to put on a big buddy act and get you up to meet my new bride and you play along with it, understand?"

He nodded vaguely, teased another drink down while I gave him a loud, descriptive picture about the delights of being a fresh bridegroom and finally got him to agree to meet the wife despite the warnings of the two older guys on my right. I paid the bill, draped my arm over his shoulder and staggered off to the elevators and pushed the button.

Angelo's seeing me was accidental, but the consternation on his face was real. He said something to the bell captain, who nodded and came over in time to step into the elevator behind us. The minute the door closed he said, "Señor?"

I dropped the act and grinned at him. "I'm okay, Angelo."

"I was worried." He glanced at Joey suspiciously.

"Friend," I said. "How's everything look?"

"Director Sabin's men are everywhere, señor. I understand he and Carlos Ortega had a falling out over his attentions to the Gordot woman, but Director Sabin is insistent. He thinks he is very much taken with her, but it is more a matter of his hating to be opposed. He calls her room regularly to make sure she is there and the guards watch her door carefully. Things are not going well."

"Quit sweating. You get that radio from Rosa Lee's?"

He bobbed his head. "Before dawn. It is already installed in a safe place for future use. An operator stands by at all times."

"Good. Keep him there."

"About the Gordot woman . . ."

"Flight 51 goes out at midnight, doesn't it?"

"That is correct, señor. The shift goes off duty here promptly at ten. We must be ready by then."

"We'll be ready by then," I said.

The car stopped at our floor and I went back into the drunk act and let Joey help me off while Angelo continued up higher. I banged on the door to the suite until Kim answered, watched her face look at me with utter disgust until she closed the door behind us, then change into one of surprise when I popped back to normal. I kept my voice loud and thick until I had the radio turned up again

and when Kim got the idea she called over the noise to
Joey to help me into the shower.

When the water was running too hard for any hidden
mikes to pick us up she said, "Who's he?"

"Joey Jolley, the one I told you about." I looked at him
and nudged him with my hand. "Let's have it, kid. What's
this bit of showing up here?"

Someplace Joey lost his grand manner. His voice was
quavery and above his normal pitch; his hands clutched
together to keep from trembling. "You stuck me, Morgan.
If I knew it was going to be like that I would have kept
out of it."

"Get to the point, Joey."

He took a breath, let it out slowly and nodded. He
looked at Kim and said, "You want her to hear it too?"

"All of it."

"Sure, Morgan." He licked his lips, folded and refolded
his hands. "I poked around like you asked me to and
picked up enough to put it together. Herm Bailey . . . he
was the one who really set me wise. I found him hiding
out in the storeroom over the Dixieland Tavern because
Whitey Tass had his boys out looking to work him over
for lousing up one of their jobs while he was drunk."

"Details, damn it!"

"I . . . I'm trying, Morgan," he said nervously. "Anyway, the way it plays out starts with Gorman Yard. He
had this guy with him for a while that Old Gussie didn't
know about. I don't know where Yard picked him up, but
that one had a feeling about guys on the lam. He kept this
guy in his room and made him pay pretty steep for the
privilege.

"Someplace along the line Yard got the idea this guy
had a lot more loot than he was carrying on him and Yard
wanted a bite of it. From what I heard he didn't want to
tackle the guy alone. He was a pretty mean type who trav-
eled with a rod and didn't mind using it. So he figures out
another angle. He wangles an introduction to Whitey Tass
and lays it in his lap. The deal was for Whitey to have his
boys pick the guy up and squeeze the location of the
cache from him.

"They had it all set up, but my guess is that Gorman
Yard got a little too cagey and the guy smelled the deal
out and took off. Naturally, this made Whitey look like a
sucker and he doesn't take that kind of thing. He blew the
whistle on Yard by putting the police wise to where he
was holed up and Yard took a fall on that upstate rap.

"It would have been okay for Yard if he had kept his big mouth shut, but in the can he sounds off about how he's going to even things with Whitey Tass and Whitey hears about it and one of his boys in the can pulls the cork on Yard at Whitey's orders and Yard's on a slab the same week.

"Nobody would've been the wiser. It was a good job, an industrial accident, the report read, but then you showed up in the neighborhood, got through to Bernice Case and started her asking questions about Yard's connection with Whitey Tass. That put him behind the eight ball again and he couldn't take any chances on what information the Case girl had so he cooled her himself."

"And that brings us up to you," I said.

"You shouldn't have asked me to do it, Morgan."

"What happened?"

Joey shuddered again and wiped the back of his hand across a dry mouth. "Whitey tumbled to me. Now he knows I've connected him with the kill on Yard and Case." His eyes looked at me hopelessly. "He followed me, Morgan. I know he was there in Miami. I thought I was clear getting into the Keys, but I'm not so sure. There was another guy I saw once at a gas station and again at a diner. He could have been one of Whitey's men."

"Nobody was on that boat with you except the captain, was there?"

"No."

"And nobody's coming this way while this hurricane is building either. If Whitey's behind you, then he's still in the States and we can nail him when we get back there."

"Morgan . . ."

"Cool it, Joey," I said. "Nobody's going to touch you here."

For the first time Kim spoke, her voice crisply curious. "Do you mind telling me what this is all about?"

I looked at her just as seriously. "About forty-million bucks floating around someplace."

An expression of incredulity crossed her face. "What?"

"I never had it, kitten."

She frowned and shook her head. "Part of the money was found in your room when you were picked up."

"That belonged to a former tenant, the guy Yard was harboring. When he took off to get away from Whitey Tass's mob he left it there. He had plenty more and it wasn't worth coming back for and I got stuck with it when they shook down my room."

Her smile had a hard edge to it. "Then explain away the three five-hundred-dollar bills in your possession."

"I told you. Casino winnings. This would be a perfect spot to unload that hot money. Ortega tried his best to make a deal with me to take care of it, so I know the outlet is available. Anybody could have brought it in. Hell, I was tagged for the job, so what did somebody else have to worry about? They'll check bills downstairs for counterfeit, but they aren't trying to match up serial numbers with stolen bills. Why should they? All they had to do was put it back in circulation again and they wouldn't be out a buck."

"Then Ortega *knows* you have it?"

"He *thinks* he knows it, baby."

She frowned again. "Somebody shot at you. Somebody tried to frame you for Rosa's death." She paused, then added, "Somebody else thinks you have it too."

"Do they?" I asked softly.

Kim looked at me, puzzled. "What do you mean?"

"Nothing. Just an idea I have." I looked at my watch. It was a quarter to six. "I don't know how long I'll be gone, so I'll lay the program out now. Think you can go it alone?"

Kim nodded hesitantly.

"Angelo has it arranged for Lisa to go out of here dressed as a maid. He'll make sure she gets to the plane. What I want you to do is get down to her room and see if you can imitate her voice and the general tone of her conversation in case Sabin should call. After the takeoff time for her flight you get back up here and stay with Joey here until I get back. Clear?"

Joey said, "What about me, Morgan?" His voice was barely audible.

"You stay here. Keep the door closed unless you're sure it's one of us."

"Morg . . . you're positive about Whitey Tass?"

"If he knows you're here he knows you can't hurt him and he won't be dumb enough to come after you until after the storm anyway." I got up from the edge of the tub and turned off the shower.

When I turned around Kim was standing there, her eyes full of confusion, staring at me as if she were looking through a microscope. "You still don't believe me, do you?" I asked her.

Her lovely face reflected the turmoil of her mind. "Why should I?"

"No reason to," I told her and walked outside.

As I reached the door I heard her quick steps behind me and her voice say, *"Morgan."*

I stopped and turned around. "What?"

She couldn't seem to say what she wanted to say. Instead, she simply shrugged. "Nothing."

I grinned at her, went into a drunk-trying-to-sober-up act and opened the door.

10

JUAN FUCILLA ENTERED the bar promptly at six. I timed my unsteady path across the lobby to intercept him and as I passed him, said, "Men's room." He was too shrewd to miss the implication or give any indication that he had heard me and continued on to the bar while I went into the john at the far end of the room. The guy in the tight tuxedo who had followed me made sure of where I was going, then went back to his original position beside the desk, scrutinizing the departing guests.

Five minutes later Fucilla joined me at the washbasins, waited until we were alone, then took the packet I had handed him. His analysis was simple but thorough, feeling the consistency of the heroin, tasting it, and inspecting it under the light through a tiny but high-powered glass. When he finished he slipped the packet in his pocket and said, "Excellent quality, señor."

"The best," I agreed.

His little eyes squinted at me. "My immediate superiors you will deal with directly think it will be a pleasure to do business with you."

"How many of them?"

"Merely two, señor. Both are very reliable officers." He coughed apologetically and fidgeted nervously with the buttons on his coat. "They, ah . . . approve of your direct methods."

"What methods?"

"Elimination of someone of no consequence who might possibly, er, hamper our business relationship with the slip of the tongue."

I didn't let it show on my face, but I knew what he meant. The little bastard thought I had knocked off Rosa Lee to cut her out of the picture altogether! For a moment the greed in his face was tempered by respect. I didn't bother to deny his assumption. At least it made him a little less difficult to deal with, thinking of what retribution he could expect if he crossed me. And he cleared up one more detail for me. If he thought I had killed Rosa, then he couldn't have done it himself.

The thread holding the chain of events jerked tighter and the probables grew closer to the possibles.

I said, "You have a car?"

"*Sí*. A new Volvo. It is outside in the parking lot."

"Go wait for me in it. It will be better if we are not seen together."

Fucilla nodded his agreement, dried his hands on some paper towels and left. I gave him a couple of minutes, waited until the two men who came in to relieve themselves had gone, then pried open the single frosted-glass window that opened on the rear courtyard, hoisted myself through it, closed it carefully, then walked down the alley that led to the street.

They had built the Rose Castle of native rock on the fingertip of the island, a strategic point overlooking the natural harbor entrance whose gun emplacements could command the entire area. The dull black snouts of the cannon were still visible, curios now, but reminders of the days when this simple little island represented an almost invulnerable power.

The facing of the ten-foot-thick wall rose up sixty feet, its sheer, smooth surface barely pockmarked with the ravages of time, the imprint of old cannon shot from ships standing offshore like little dimples in its face. The primary purpose of the bastion had been to repel an attack from the sea, so except for ventilation slits, there were no openings in the sides. The cannons had been fired from the top of the wall, giving them the advantage in sighting and trajectory in long-range gunnery, the reefs surrounding the position making a landing by small boats so hazardous it was virtually impossible.

A new two-lane coquina roadbed led up to the main gate of the Rose Castle, splitting into a half-moon a fenced-off promenade that allowed visitors an excellent view of the structure. But beyond, the road narrowed to a single-lane graveled drive through a wrought-iron gate guarded by a sentry in an ornate booth.

I didn't have to see it. The briefing Carter and Rice had given me along with recent photographs of the place imprinted the picture vividly in my mind. Nor did inanimate objects raise any problem. The only thing that could negate the situation was the security arrangement.

Juan Fucilla beeped his horn at the guard and was admitted without question, the man not even bothering to scrutinize me. Evidently the money tree had pretty long roots and they were watered right down to their very ends.

From the guard post to the walls was another two hundred yards and before we reached the gate I heard someone sneeze in the darkness and knew the grounds were patrolled.

Next to me, Fucilla said, "Ordinarily the Castle is lit with floodlights, señor. For the benefit of the visitors of course. It is quite a beautiful sight."

"Why is it blanked out now?"

"The approaching storm, my friend. The wiring has a fault. The last time it happened a short circuit blacked out all of Nuevo Cádiz. In emergencies the Castle operates its own generator to supply immediate power."

"Clever," I said.

"Ah, yes. Señor Carlos Ortega has thoroughly modernized our country."

The headlights of the car swung through a turn, then threw their beams against the vast expanse of the dismal gray structure. Unlike the other three sides that flanked the ocean, this one was not devoted to military functionalism. No attack could be expected from this end, and the gaping mouth of the entrance and the large rectangular windows were decorated with ornate carvings and stone images of long-dead heroes set into niches in the granite. Every window was covered with iron gratings set into the rock, the main gate protected by a wrist-thick grillework that seemed impregnable.

Juan parked the car next to a battered Ford and a new Volkswagen, waved me out and we both walked up the stone path to the gate. Behind it, a pair of armed guards flashed lights in our faces, responded to his order and one moved away to trip a lever that sent the metal gate sliding upward to admit us before it clanged down again.

I was finally inside the Rose Castle.

Carter and Rice had done their research well. I matched the details of the place with those in my memory, making note of late renovations and the possible reasons for their uses. Luckily, Fucilla had a strange sense of pride and insisted on giving me a guided tour of the section previously used as housing accommodations for the officers before leading me to the large mahogany-paneled office to meet his superiors.

Captain Ramero and Lieutenant Valente were all too

glad to shake hands with someone who was going to in-
crease their personal fortunes. Each made a thorough inspection of the packet Juan handed them, asked him if I
understood their language, and when he assured them I
was very much just another American gangster with no
such possibility, discussed how much they were going to
be able to cut the stuff without losing its effectiveness and
what the payoff was to be.

Both of them accepted Fucilla's deal and even understood why I insisted on seeing the prospective customers.
Captain Ramero looked at his watch and told Fucilla, "I
suggest you get through with it, then. Always when these
damnable emergencies arise Señor Sabin makes a personal
inspection of the place and, although he takes the money,
he wouldn't approve of us having him do what he de-
mands."

"It will not take long," Fucilla assured him.

The captain turned to me, an oily smile on his face.
"Tell me, señor, when are you prepared to make your first
delivery?"

I studied his face briefly, spotted the attention both the
lieutenant and Fucilla were giving me and said, "Oh, a
week, two weeks. I'm kind of on a honeymoon."

There was a brief exchange of glances between them
and I knew I had guessed it right. Their present supply
was critically short.

I said, "But if you need it I can get it to you fast. In
that case it had better be damn fast, because if this hurricane clobbers us there's no telling what will happen."

"Your supply . . . it is in a safe place?"

"Not against a hurricane."

"Then perhaps it would be better if it were delivered
here."

I shook my head. "I want payment on delivery, Captain."

"That can be arranged."

"Good."

"It is done. How much can you supply and at what
price?"

"Two kilos and you're getting a break. Twenty grand
for the lot." I saw the surprised expression on his face that
disappeared almost before it was born and added, "Sure it's
cheap. You'll have enough to last you the lifetime of your
customers here and plenty to peddle someplace else. If you
want it cold, it's hijacked junk and the guys who carried it
are dead. Nobody is left to talk and nobody knows where

it went to. The only thing I want is clean, spendable U.S. dollars out of the deal and twenty thousand untaxed dollars will do me nicely."

The captain's smile had an even oilier slick now. His half-bow was almost gracious. And if he thought I wasn't reading his mind he was crazy. Once he got his hands on those two kilos I was just another dead American gangster, possibly lost in the hurricane, and the twenty grand he'd have to raise to show me would stick right in his pocket along with all that lovely profit from the sale of the stuff. I had hung out a juicy chunk of bait and it was gulped down without a thought.

"An excellent arrangement," he said. "When can we expect it?"

"I'll have to get back to the city . . ."

He waved it off as inconsequential. "Señor Fucilla's car is at your disposal. I suggest we complete our transaction immediately."

"What about the cash?"

"It will be available upon your return."

"You got guards outside . . ." I started.

"They will be instructed to let you pass."

"Okay, sounds good. If it works out maybe we can do business again."

His friendly laugh was as humorless as a dry bone. "Of course, señor. It is a pleasure to be engaged in a profitable trade." But what he really meant was that he took me for a one-shot hood who came up lucky on a job and who didn't have a chance in the world of making it on a second try. The walls of the Rose Castle were nice and high and the waters at their base were populated with enough scavenger sharks to dispose of a body quickly and efficiently.

The captain looked at Fucilla. "Now, our friend would like to see our . . . guests."

Fucilla returned his bow. "With pleasure. This way, señor."

The lights of Nuevo Cádiz threw a dull glow against the low-hanging clouds above it. I turned the Volvo off the coquina road to the narrow macadam highway that led toward it, passing the ancient vehicles rattling toward the safety of the city. The night air was more humid now, sweeping in with cough-like gusts.

Someplace out over the ocean the swirling force of the storm was gathering its forces together, getting ready to pounce. Right now it was sitting back like a gourmet surveying the delicacies he was going to eat, savoring the aroma and enjoying the excitement of the impending meal.

I ran over the layout of the Rose Castle in my mind again, positioning the guards, their attitudes, remembering the corridors and stairways dimly lit by an inadequate generating system that led to the new maximum-security section.

Whoever had contracted for the renovations had found the ancient granite walls too heavy to break through, so the aluminum conduit carrying the power lines had been laid along steel spikes driven into the masonry between the blocks.

Juan Fucilla had not noticed me tracing its course until we came to the intersection where the overhead line ran into a junction box at the top of a vertical pipe that ran through the floor. He had been too busy giving me details of the Rose Castle's historical background, proudly pointing out features of its impregnability and talking of its reknowned prisoners in the past and the abortive attempts to rescue them.

I had played the interested tourist to the hilt and asked him what lay below the level we were on and he had smiled pompously because I was his co-conspirator and said, "Ah, señor, that is something reserved for official eyes only. It is part of the past we have brought back to life more than once. Our ancestors were very ingenious people who knew how to deal with their enemies."

"Oh?" I made like I didn't understand and he smiled again.

"The more naïve refer to it as the dungeon . . . the torture chamber. We prefer to call it the interrogation section. It is very effective. Even the sight of it has eliminated the necessity of lengthy discussions with our, ah, guests."

"Smart, buddy," I told him. "Any chance of seeing it?"

Fucilla chuckled as if he were enjoying a joke. "Well . . . since you are here on business that has, let's say, official sanction, why not?" His eyes half closed, but he kept smiling. "It might even be a good idea, a reminder that our relationship should always be, say . . . honest?"

I grinned at his veiled threat and waved to him to lead the way.

The opening had been designed to resist a hasty search for it. Fucilla passed it deliberately to prove the point, paused and escorted me back a few yards and pointed to the space between two massive beams supporting the over-head. He reached up, partially withdrew two of the huge bolts studding the beam and pushed against the granite wall. Somewhere a counterbalance creaked on its pulleys and the slab swung in ponderously.

Modern horror movies had a basis in fact, but they had never gone far enough. The devices they had built into the Rose Castle hundreds of years ago were even more sophisticated than those the Nazis designed. Even then they had known about tolerance levels for pain and invented machines that could break any human's endurance. There were implements whose purpose was so apparent that any woman seeing them would go into hysteria. What they had thought of to do to a male even gave me a squeamish feeling in my stomach and I was there as a guest. But they had been neat about it. Blood troughs and receptacles were all at hand to protect the interrogators, and wooden benches and tables were placed for the benefit of audience participation.

It was all very interesting and I nodded in rapt appreciation at Fucilla's vivid description of each piece of equipment. But what I was really interested in was our progress through the rooms to the one whose heavy door muffled the steady *thump-thump* of a gasoline engine turning over a generator.

When we had completed the tour and the grim look on my face satisfied Fucilla, we retraced our steps and went back up the hand-hewed staircase to the landing where Fucilla pushed down a locking handle in the beam and pulled the granite slab inward with the iron ring built into its face.

"Now then," he had said, "We will see those we came to see."

There had been twelve of them held there, each in his own room behind solid wooden doors with an inch-wide peephole built into it to check on the occupant. The quarters had been furnished lavishly for a prison, more like one-room apartments than like normal cells. But these were political prisoners and the intent was a psychological one. It kept them from realizing their true status, allowing them to maintain a futile hope in the midst of despair. Once they were subjugated to narcotics, control was complete. Alive, they were a source of revenue or political advantage, always available for negotiation, forced to act as Ortega wished them to unless they wanted to suffer the pain and possible death of narcotics withdrawal.

Victor Sable had surprised me. Prison life had barely touched him at all. He had been sitting at his desk writing in longhand, his face in serious thought. Except for a slight balding, he matched the photos I had seen. There was no doubting his identity. The single light bulb had thrown his face into sharp relief and I had recognized both profile and front-face views.

I had deliberately taken a certain amount of time inspecting each prisoner so that when I reached Sable nothing was unusual, but once having recognized him I was more concerned with the locks on the door than I was the man inside. When I was satisfied, I had passed on to the next room and the next, without Fucilla ever realizing what I had come for.

If only the weather would hold off, I thought. Absently, I remembered Miami Advisory had named her Frances.

I parked the Volvo in the hotel lot at eleven fifteen, lost myself in the traffic that was going in and out of the main doors and got myself a place at the crowded end of the bar. It took another ten minutes before one of the casino guards spotted me, walked over and spoke hurriedly to the one near the desk, who looked my way with a confused frown and decided to see what was going on.

I made a point of ignoring him while he edged in next to me and ordered a drink. He finally turned and said, "You have been enjoying yourself, señor?"

"In a way."

"We have missed you at the tables."

"I was sick." I let out a shudder to prove the point. "I got me some fresh air. Feel a lot better now."

He was glad enough to see me back without pressing the point. "Perhaps it would be better if you slept."

I finished my drink and put the glass back on the bar. "You may be right at that," I said. I told him good night and reached the elevators. In the reflection of the glass over the calendar of events I could see him still watching my back, the bar phone at his ear to alert the guard on my floor that I was coming up.

As I touched the button I heard the whine of a siren clearing a path to the front door. Four of the bellboys pulled themselves away from their conclave at the desk and hurried outside. The few of us waiting for the elevator stepped back to see what it was all about and watched while the doors were pushed inward and five men followed by an assortment of crisp, efficient-looking women entered, the bellhops trailing with red-and-white foot lockers.

The man next to me said, "They finally got here."

"Who?"

"Volunteer medics from Miami."

"They're setting up an emergency field hospital. One thing this place hasn't got and that's enough doctors. Those guys have a lot of guts." He grinned at me. "They could have brought some better-looking nurses."

"What are they doing here?"

"You hear a late advisory?"

"Damn right. Those slobs have been holding it back, but somebody passed the word that it's closer than they're letting on. I'm damn glad I'm getting out. This blow's got trouble in it. The next flight's the last one leaving. After that it's storm-shelter time."

"You sure about that next flight?"

He gave a serious twist of his head. "Check with the desk. Everything else is canceled out." He looked at me curiously. "You on it?"

"No."

"Tough," he said.

I looked at the group going past me, their faces grimly professional. One was in his late twenties and three were well past middle age. All of the women were in their middle thirties. But one of the men had a grim professional look and he wasn't a doctor. His expensive gray suit was well tailored to his hulking form, the snap-brim of the fedora half shading his eyes. He carried the trench coat over his arm in a practiced way that looked natural, but put his hand near the gun he always carried. He didn't hurry. He didn't have to. What he came for was still here and not about to leave.

I said his name silently, feeling it roll across my tongue, tasting the sensation of killing him. *The man was Whitey Tass.*

At the fifth floor I got out alone and walked down the corridor toward my room. At the other end the lone sentry trying so hard to be a part of the scenery saw me and turned away casually to resume his aimless strolling. I rapped on the door, heard a startled grunt and feet cross the room. A muffled voice said, "Yes?"

"Morg. Open up."

Joey Jolley had almost gone to pieces. His face was drained of color and his hands were too shaky to throw the bolt in place, so I had to do it for him. Inside, the radio was blaring away with loud, cheerful music.

I looked at my watch. It was five after twelve.

"Where's Kim?" I motioned for him to keep his voice down.

"She . . . did what you told her to. She's still there."

This time I had to take the chance that they were too busy to monitor my phone. I dialed Lisa's room, heard it ring twice before it was picked up and a listless voice answered with a hello. I said, "Morg, kitten. Come on home," then hung up.

I looked at my watch again and the hands seemed to be double-timing around the dial. Somehow, Kim had made her own way to Lisa's room unobserved and somehow she'd make it back. However she pulled the guard off balance was her own affair, but I couldn't afford the waste of even a minute.

Once more I had to hope Lady Luck was riding my horse. I picked up the phone and dialed Room 203. After it rang a half-dozen times a pleasant voice answered with *"Si?"*

"Luis Rondo?" I asked in English.

"Yes," he answered, "this is he."

"My name is Winters, Mr. Rondo. Your services have been recommended to me by a friend."

"Ah, yes," he said noncommittally.

"I want to indulge myself in a hobby," I told him. "That of flying."

For a moment there was silence and I knew he was weighing the situation and balancing it out. "Since you are in the import business I was wondering if you could order me a plane."

"Yes, that is possible. Have you anything specific in mind?"

"Oh, something fast. One that could hold five or six people."

"I see."

"How quickly could it be delivered?"

"That depends on how quickly you want it."

I laughed, faking a joke. "Like right away. Once I want something I get impatient until it's in my hands."

He played the game with me. "Of course, I understand. With such a customer I wish I could deliver it before the sun rose. However . . ."

"Do the best you can, okay?"

"By all means, sir. In fact, I have a party in Miami with a Queenaire for sale. At the earliest opportunity I will contact him for you, Mr. Winters. I appreciate your call. Will I be able to reach you at your room?"

"I'll be here."

"Well, I will do what I can."

I hung up and went to the window overlooking the street. Most of the windows on street level were boarded over and only stray lines of light seeped out onto the sidewalks. The clusters of people below were still milling about, not certain where to go. Since the danger wasn't immediate yet there was a mock carnival atmosphere about the scene. The breeze had turned cool finally, a welcome relief, and they were enjoying it while they could, the sounds of guitar music and singing coming up through the happy confusion.

Joey sidled up next to me, his face drawn. "What do we do now?"

"Wait," I told him, then grabbed the phone again and asked for Angelo. When he came on I told him to bring me a pot of coffee with a couple of sandwiches.

Ten minutes later I let him in and while he was unloading his tray said, "I need two kilo-size cardboard containers filled with confectioners' sugar. Wrap them in plastic and seal them with tape. Can do?"

Angelo nodded. "Yes, we have such in the kitchen."

"Outside in the lot is a new Volvo. There's a dent in the front-right fender so you can't miss it. Stick them under the front seat."

He frowned, but didn't question my motives.

"Did you get through to Jose?"

"*Sí*. He was reached by radio. Your boat is still waiting, but there is little time remaining."

"Stay in touch with him. I'll call you when I can to see how we're going to handle this."

"Please be careful, señor."

I let him out, closed the door and glanced at my watch again. It was twelve twenty. Overhead I heard the throb of heavy engines that grew into a roar as the plane passed almost directly over the hotel before turning to the northwest. I said, "Luck, Lisa," and made myself a drink, then sat down to wait some more.

11

KIM GOT BACK at twelve thirty, using her key and slipping through the door to close it silently behind her. She gave me the okay sign with thumb and forefinger, listened to see if there was anyone behind her in the hall, then with a sigh of relief went over and made herself a quick drink.

"Give it to me," I told her.

"She got off the way you planned it. Russo Sabin called just before I left the room, so he doesn't know about it yet." She smiled at me like a conspirator. "But he will soon."

"Why?"

"He's been calling every fifteen minutes to check on her.

"Now the stuff really hits the fan," I said. "He'll turn this hotel inside out. There aren't any more flights out so he'll think she's in the area and will spread his men out to find her.

"Morgan . . ."

"What?"

"Supposing he holds you on suspicion?"

Before I could answer her the phone rang. I picked it up and said, "Hello." The voice on the other end was Luis Rondo and he said in a businesslike manner, "Mr. Winters, I believe I can fill your order according to your specifications."

"Confirmed?"

"Yes, quite. Delivery will be made at the time you suggested, north end. The owner wishes to make a quick turnover, so there won't be much time to bargain."

"I understand. Thanks for your attention."

"Certainly, señor."

When I put the phone back Kim asked softly, "Who was that?"

My voice was almost drowned out in the blaring of the radio. "Rondo. He made a contact with Miami. Your agency's sending a plane out to pick us up at the north

145

end of the airfield at dawn." I glanced at my watch. "Now we can move." Over her shoulder I saw Joey Jolley, out of earshot, making himself another drink. "Whitey Tass came in on that last plane out of Miami. Don't let Joey know about it or he's liable to panic. You're to stay with him all the way. Just keep Joey out of sight until I get back."

Those big dark eyes roamed my face before they dug into my own. "And if you don't?"

"You two get on that plane and cut out. It means I won't be coming back."

"My orders . . ."

"Screw your orders, doll. I'm making command decisions at this point. I'll tell you this much: I can get into the Rose Castle and I may be able to get out. If I don't it's because I'm dead. But if I go you won't have to worry about Victor Sable anymore because he'll take the big fall with me."

"You'll kill him?"

"I won't have to. They'll do it for me. They couldn't afford to have either of us alive after this. At least we know he's alive at this point so that much of the mission is accomplished. Either way your report will be positive."

Her hand touched my arm and something changed in her voice. "Morgan . . . what are the chances?"

I looked down into the depths of her eyes. Seriously, I said, "You either survive or you don't, sugar. At least I'm a positive thinker. Let's leave it at that."

"You will be . . . careful?"

"Since when do you care?"

She stiffened as if I had slapped her, the cold professional attitude wiping out any trace of feminine concern, and that was the way I wanted it. It was a cold, nasty business and you had to keep it that way to keep alive.

All she said was, "I care about the success of the project."

"Then make sure somebody turns in the report."

"I will."

"Good. Now get into your traveling clothes and don't carry anything more than you can put in your handbag. The guard outside is stationed at the end of the corridor. I'm going to fake him out long enough for you two to get down the stairs to the lobby. There ough to be enough of a crowd to cover you if you play it right. Stay casual and play it straight. There's a Volvo in the parking lot about halfway down from the entrance. Make sure nobody sees

you; get in and stay in the back seat below window level.
When I'm clear I'll get you out to the airfield." I looked
over to make sure Joey couldn't see me and said, "Don't
let Whitey Tass spot him."

Kim memorized the description I gave her of Whitey
and nodded. "Would he know Joey was here?"

"No, but Joey doesn't know he's here either. Since
they're setting up a field hospital downstairs the hotel will
probably be headquarters for any evacuees and they'll be
herding all the foreign nationals in. Don't play Whitey
down. He's an old hand at this, with a damn big personal
interest at stake. He'll have every entrance covered somehow. You'll just have to pick the right time and place."

"Very well."

I went over and dug the bills out from under the carpet
and shoved them in my pocket. Cash always has a way of
talking its own language and you never know when you
need it to speak for you. I stuck the extra .45 clips along
with a handful of spare cartridges in my other pocket,
cautioned Joey to be as inconspicuous as possible and left.

Taking care of the guard was a simple matter of walking past him, cutting down the west wing into the adjoin-
ing hall and knocking on the door of an empty room
while he watched curiously. After standing there five minutes I shrugged, and went back to where I came from,
walked to the elevator and stepped in when the door
opened. They'd pick me up again downstairs, but as long
as they had me in sight, that was all that mattered.

The atmosphere in the casino had changed. Those who
couldn't leave had a resigned attitude and were more concerned with having a good time to forget their troubles
than they were with gambling. The same crowd still
played the tables, coolly indifferent to the horde of natives
who watched them with amazement, gaping at the money
changing hands in amounts bigger than they had ever seen
in their lives.

From my spot at the bar I cased the room carefully,
picked out some of Russo Sabin's men and the lean form
of Major Turez. If Whitey Tass was around he had concealed himself pretty well. It could well have been that he
was locked in a room somewhere, not worried about locat-
ing Joey Jolley because nobody was leaving the place, figuring to run him down in the turmoil of the storm. It was
a safe bet that he would have registered with a phony
passport under another name, and with all the disorder at
the desk the clerk couldn't verify a description of him.

I didn't see Angelo until he was beside me paging a Mr. Roberts at the bar. Between calls he hissed, "The boat has left, señor. There was nothing else for him to do."

"It's okay, kid. Thanks." I said it without moving my lips or looking at him. He kept calling for Mr. Roberts and on the way back past me again I said, "The girl?"

"She made the flight. Be alert, señor. Director Sabin is in the hotel. He knows she is gone." That was all he had time for. He kept up his paging into the casino area until he was buried in the crowd.

I finished my drink slowly, waved off the refill and walked toward the crap tables. The cashier changed two hundred dollars into chips for me and I played them off a few at a time, picking my way to the end of the room. The guards had me spotted and let me pass as long as I was in sight, but before I reached the last table I saw the major wave to them, pull four out of the ranks to hurry over to the desk.

That left only one standing by the door leading to the service bar and when I sank the stiffened tips of my fingers deep into his gut he never knew what hit him. I had him through the doors and on the floor without anyone seeing us leave and when I brought the butt end of the .45 down across his skull it was going to be a long day before he woke up again.

I dragged him behind the bar, shoved him into the storage space there and slammed the sliding doors shut. When it was done I got up and walked through the kitchen and out into the alley behind the hotel. The dozen cooks and helpers who saw me go were too busy to bother me and didn't think I was any of their business anyway.

You could smell the storm now. It had a fresh, salty tang, coming in on a steady wind whose intensity had increased steadily. It still wasn't strong enough to blow more than loose papers around, but a hurricane was a compact thing that always arrived unexpectedly no matter how much warning it gave. It would come in with the sudden, devastating fury of an explosion, create its destruction and pass on with blue skies and sunny days to bury the dead on.

The alley led out to the far end of the parking lot in back of the parapet that encircled it. I took it at a trot, pushed my way through the matted tropical vegetation that decorated its extremity and hugged the space between the parked cars and the wall, running toward the Volvo.

I almost didn't make it in time.

They were just a formless blur in the darkness at first, seeming to sway gently and merge with the wind-driven shadows from the banana trees and palms behind them. Then I saw the ivory glow of Kim's legs as she lay sprawled on the ground face down, her skirt whipped up to her hips.

I ran then, half tripping over unseen obstacles in the way, seeing the white ovals of two faces whose bodies were locked in a deadly struggle, and the .45 jumped into my hand. I let out a strangled yell when I saw the terror in Joey's eyes as he was losing the fight to keep Whitey Tass's hand from bringing his gun into line with his head. One car had jumped the short curbing into the grassy lane and I had to scramble over the hood before I reached them and I knew I wasn't going to be able to make it. Whitey's teeth were bared in a grimace of pure pleasure as he brought the gun around and there wasn't one thing I could do about it except watch.

But somebody else was watching too. I heard the sharp crack of a small-caliber weapon, saw the tiny flash of flame from the top of the parapet fifty feet away and the tableau froze into position even as I brought the .45 up and blasted two shots at the source of the gunfire. Then Whitey Tass seemed to melt slowly and collapse in a heap at Joey's feet.

He was too terror-ridden to talk when I reached him. I turned Kim over, saw the bruise on her forehead and the flutter of her eyes, picked her up in my arms and nudged Joey into the Volvo, tossing Kim in beside him. Somebody had started yelling at the front of the hotel and in another minute the place was going to be swarming with police.

Whitey I didn't have to worry about anymore. That single shot had taken him right through his ear and he died so quickly only one drop of blood marked the bullet entry. I grabbed the gun out of his hand, climbed behind the wheel of the Volvo and spun it out of the parking slot, shifted into forward even as I saw the crowd in the rear-view mirror running toward us. I cut down the ramp, turned east when I hit the street and gave the Volvo all it would take. As I made the first corner I thought I saw other cars taking up the chase, but I couldn't be sure.

Luckily, traffic coming into the city had all but ceased. A few stragglers still drifted along the shoulders of the road, the headlights of the car warning them of our approach. I wasn't familiar with this section of the city at all, but in the distance I could see the revolving beacon of the airfield sweeping the sky at intermittent intervals, and headed in that direction, hoping I wasn't going to trap myself in any dead-end streets.

Beside me, Kim stirred, groaned softly and lifted her hand to her head. Joey's breath was coming in gasps and when I said, "What the hell happened?" he could hardly speak for a minute.

"I . . . don't know. It . . . was Whitey Tass."

"Yeah, I know."

"Is he. . .?"

"Dead," I finished.

Joe choked on a sob of relief. Kim came out of it then, sizing up our position quickly. She pushed herself upright, her teeth clamped against the pain. I didn't have to ask her anything. Her words came out clipped but concise.

"I didn't think anybody saw us. At least the guards didn't. We . . . reached the parking lot. Some people were there . . . getting out of a car . . . so we hid ourselves in the bushes. My fault . . . because I wasn't watching . . . all areas. Concerned about . . . those people. He came up from behind and when I . . . went for my gun he hit me with his."

Joey had composed himself enough to sound rational again. "He was going to kill me, Morgan. If he hadn't swung on her he would have. I just grabbed his arm, that's all. He was too strong. He laughed at me. He was almost ready to shoot me and he was laughing about it."

Kim said, "Did you kill him, Morgan?"

"No."

I saw her frown, her hand coming away from her face. "Then who. . ."

"The shot came from the top of the parapet. Somebody else followed you out too."

"Sabin's people?" she whispered.

I shook my head. "No."

The anger in her put a bite in her voice. "*Who, Morgan?*"

"It's just beginning to figure out," I said. "That shot came from a peculiar place. Joey's back almost obscured Whitey's and even a wild shot had more of a chance of hitting him than Whitey."

"What are you getting to?"

"That shot was a perfect, direct hit. It was meant for Whitey. The next two would have picked you off the same way if I hadn't blasted a couple into his position."

"Morgan. . ."

"When I'm sure, you'll know about it."

I wrenched the car around another turn, the tires screeching a wild protest. The tail end slued around in the gravel before taking hold, then I gassed it down the dirt road in front of me. In the mirror I could see the reflection of other headlights against the low-hanging scud; then they passed, missing the turnoff I had chosen. There was only a half mile to go and I knew they'd be doubling back looking for my exit route when they missed me.

I saw the turn coming up, braked, downshifted, and threw the wheel over. I heard Kim's half-scream as she saw it the same time I did and I had just enough control left to avoid it. Somebody had abandoned a two-wheeled wagon almost in the middle of the road and it had damned near creamed us.

At the least it could do the job right if anybody was on our tail. I jammed my foot on the brake, backed up and hopped out. It took only a few seconds to grab the wagon by its tongue and pull it another four feet out into the road before I was back at the wheel, with the airport directly ahead.

They had the time; I didn't. I dropped them at the south end of the runway, and getting back to the other end would be up to them. When they got out Kim turned and leaned in the window, her lovely hair in disarray over her face, but eyes vitally alive and a mouth, lusher than ever, framing a statement.

"Morgan," she said, "be careful. I really do care."

I kissed her then, just once and quickly, let out a short laugh of pleasure and threw the car into gear.

This time I knew where I was. Ten minutes later I intersected the highway, followed the signs to the coquina road leading to the Rose Castle and turned down it. Up ahead was the end of the mission.

At the gate, the guard admitted me without question. Another pair on patrol around the grounds merely nodded when I parked the car, then went off on their assigned route. I reached under the seat, found the two containers Angelo had left there for me, picked them out and stuck them in the bushes under one of the stained-glass windows.

Now I was ready.

So were they. The metal grating was already up, the guards awaiting me. One said, "You will follow me, please, señor," and I nodded. But I was watching the other one to see where he located the switch that activated the grate. It was in a small metal receptacle attached to a supporting column and when he touched it I heard the grinding of gears as the thing slid down into place.

The three of them were waiting for me, Fucilla and his two superiors. Their wineglasses were full, the huge decanter on the desk half empty, and I could tell by their expressions that they had taken on a damn good load while they waited for me. My delay and the thought of having Russo Sabin walk in at any moment had them on edge and the smiles they forced were more of malice than relief.

Pomp and ceremony were demanded for the occasion and all of them were resplendent in their military uniforms heavy with braid and medals. Here rank was evident by the weight of their ornaments, the captain a real fruit-salad type, the lieutenant a little less decorated, and Fucilla, as head guard, sporting only a few awards. Each wore a Sam Browne belt with a polished holster at his hip, the gun butts protruding from one end.

The captain waved the guard away after he admitted me and leaned back in his chair. "Ah, Señor Winters." His voice was too smooth.

I answered the question before he asked it. "They evacuated the place where I kept the stuff. I had a hell of a time getting in."

"But you *do* have it? "His eyes scanned me closely, noting that it wasn't on my person."

"Certainly."

"Well, then?"

"All I want to see is the color of your money, Captain."

They let out a little chuckle all around. This attitude they could understand. In fact, the captain must have anticipated it because he rose from his chair, bowed curtly and went to the wall, pushed back a picture and spun the dial of the wall safe behind it. He found what he wanted and laid it on the desk where I could see it.

"There, señor. Twenty thousand dollars in United States currency."

I counted it slowly. It was all there. I put it back on the desk. "I left the stuff in the bushes outside the window. Look in front of the Volvo."

The captain gave me another small smile, but his eyes flocked to the other two and he said, "Lieutenant, if you please. . .?"

"With pleasure, sir." The lieutenant put his glass down

carefully on the polished desk top, smiled at me and walked to the heavy door behind us.

And that eliminated one. The odds weren't so bad now, but it had to be fast.

I reached for the twenty grand and stuck it in my coat pocket. I was getting to be a walking bank.

The captain shook his head. "Perhaps we should wait for the lieutenant's return first, señor."

"Why?" I gave him a grin and knew what he was seeing because I could feel it on my face. "You have a thing about taking money off a dead body?"

Maybe they were stupid enough to think that they were going to get away with it. Maybe they thought they had the odds on their side. They were so set to have their cake and eat it too that they never considered a cross and when it hit them they went for the guns at their sides and suddenly realized just how far the odds were against them. They never should have kept them holstered.

My first shot took the captain in the bridge of his nose, and I spun, took two quick steps to the right as Fucilla was clearing the leather and planted one square in the middle of his chest, the impact of the .45 driving him back to crash into the ornate sideboard and bring a shower of glassware down around his head. The echo of the shots still reverberated in the room like the thunder of kettledrums, the stink of cordite sharp in my nose. I had to hope the thickness of the walls and doors was enough to muffle the blast, but if it hadn't I was ready to cover both entrances and shoot my way through anybody who came in.

Those ancient Spaniards had built the Rose Castle well. A full minute passed and the only company I had was the death-glazed eyes of the captain and of Juan Fucilla. Until the lieutenant arrived and let himself in.

At first he didn't see the two on the floor. Then the smell reached him and his eyes centered on the .45 in my fist before they swept the area and realized what had happened. He didn't want to make their mistake and his expression was one of sickly pleading when he looked back at me again.

"You can drop that stuff," I told him. "It's only sugar."

He let the containers fall from his hands.

"Over here and turn around."

Eyes full of fear bulged over a slack jaw as he did as he was told. He thought he was going to be shot on the spot and his body twitched spasmodically. All he could get out was "Please, señor . . ."

"Shut up," I said. I yanked his gun out of the holster, dumped the shells out of the clip and made sure the chamber was empty before sticking it back in the holster again. He couldn't figure out what I was doing until I asked, "Who holds the keys to Victor Sable's cell?"

Then he gasped and shook his head. "Not I, señor. They are . . . in the possession of Señor Carlos Ortega only." I nudged him a little harder with the .45 and his voice became a near-shriek. "It is true, señor. There are no keys here. He was not to be moved except on Señor Ortega's orders. Only then when he is questioned is the door opened."

He was too shaken up to be lying, so I had to go along with him. I said, "Now I'm going to tell you this only once. All you have to do is make one little mistake and I'm going to put a hole in you big enough to throw a cat through without touching the sides. Is that understood?"

"*Sí*, señor." His head nodded in vigorous acknowledgment. "I . . . understand."

"Very well," I told him. "You're taking me to Sable's cell and if there's any question, it's on the captain's orders. I'm going to walk a little ahead of you and this gun is going to be right where I can get at it before you can bat an eye, so if you try one funny move you've had it."

The lieutenant tried to swallow, but his mouth was too dry, so he just nodded again. He turned his head and I could see the fear in his eyes. He was wondering what was going to happen when I was finished doing what I came to do. One thing I couldn't afford was having him go past the other guards shaking with terror.

"One more thing and consider this carefully. I don't know you and I don't give a damn about you one way or another. Whether I kill you or not depends on you. Frankly, I don't think you really give a hoot about anybody in this place yourself, so if you want to stay alive, play it square. If I get out I'll leave you with nothing more than a lump on your head and everybody will think you're a hero. They won't know whether I shot these other two before or after I got Sable out and your story can be that you acted on the captain's orders to let me view his prisoner, then I kept you under a gun and killed the captain and Fucilla on the way out. You tried to stop me and I knocked you out. Hell, they might even put you in as head man here. Got that?"

It was the last thing I told him that did the trick. He could visualize the whole picture and it looked good to him, especially the part of sitting in that big chair behind the desk himself. This time his nod was slow and deliberate. The only ones who would take the blame were dead. He was about to be a hero.

12

ONCE A PATTERN is set it is easy to accept it. The guards stationed at each vantage point had seen me go by once before with Juan Fucilla and what had been a question in their eyes before at the irregularity in the procedure now was simply complacency. Who were they to question the motives of their superiors, especially an officer of great authority? Only one of the older ones, whose lean, scarred face showed that he had been through the trouble times, contained any doubt, but it was shrouded in the cynicism that meant the grapevine had passed the word on higher echelon activities which he personally scorned, but was forced to tolerate. He looked at the lieutenant with openly hostile eyes and admitted us through the steel gate only after a careful study of the pass he had written under the captain's signature.

I didn't have to coax the lieutenant at all. He was seeing bigger things and was fitting himself into the role perfectly, staying a step behind me and a little to my left so I could see him plainly, purposely carrying on a pleasant running conversation that made us seem like old-time friends. Back in the office were two dead men that nothing could be done about anyway, except to take advantage of them. My mission didn't concern him personally in the least and there was no value in his death at all, so playing my game was the best way out with the greatest reward, and he seemed almost anxious to be cooperative.

The guard at the last post was the only one who showed any curiosity at all. Down this far in the bowels of the Rose Castle, anything that broke the monotony of the night was something to be enjoyed. He watched us go past, half turned in his seat to see what we were doing, his ears alert to catch every word.

A barked command from the lieutenant brought him to his feet and a sharp order to bring a glass of water sent him scurrying out of sight while I fingered the picklocks out of my pocket and went to work on the door of Victor Sable's cell.

Both my hands were busy and if he had wanted to jump me it would have been the time and he knew it, but he simply smiled, moved away a few feet and watched while I started manipulating the tumblers.

From inside a querulous voice said, "Yes . . . who is there?"

I stopped for a moment, opened the peephole and spoke through it. "Quiet down. We're breaking you out of here."

There was a startled intake of breath, then: "Who . . . are . . . you?"

If he even indicated a refusal I was going to kill him. I said, "I represent the United States Government."

His little cry of elation was enough. I went back to work on the locks again. I had the first one open in two minutes, was interrupted by the guard bringing the water while I faked looking through the peephole for his benefit before the lieutenant sent him off on another errand.

The other two locks took a little longer. One of the picks broke in my fingers and I had to fish the remnant of the metal out of the lock before I could continue. When that one opened, the guard had returned and taken his place at his desk.

Softly, the lieutenant asked, "How long, señor?"

"A few minutes if I'm lucky." There was an expectant look on his face.

"Something must be done about that guard, Señor. He is armed and stupid enough to interfere. He knows I have no keys to this cell."

I knew what he meant. I left the pick in the lock with most of the tumblers already fallen and made like I was ready to walk back out with him. The guard saw us coming, a note of regret in his fatuous smile because now he would be alone again.

But it didn't last long. Just as we reached him I twisted, grabbed the lieutenant's arm and threw him against the desk, spilling the guard to his knees, the gun in my hand where he could see it. Instinct made the guard grab for the pistol at his belt, but the lieutenant was still in the game and his struggle to get to his feet knocked the guy's hand away intentionally so I could bring the barrel of the .45 down against his skull and stretch him out on the floor with only the story of the lieutenant's heroic struggle to subdue me still in his memory.

When I stepped back he said, "An excellent perform-ance, señor," then smiled because I was still careful enough to watch him, knowing he was thinking the same thing I was. He could be an even greater hero if he stopped the action and nailed me too. There was just that one wall in between and he could see it. Even in his uniform with all the medals, he was still a rank amateur and I was a hard-assed pro with two kills he already knew about and just as ready to kill again. He smiled indulgently, took his place in front of me this time and let me finish opening the final lock on Victor Sable's cell.

I looked at the man standing there, wondering just what he could contribute to national security that made his safety so important. There was nothing exceptional about his appearance at all. Time had left its mark on him, but hadn't erased the dignity from his posture or the intelligence from his eyes.

He was sniffling, his body reacting to an order from his mind to control a sneeze, and when he saw me frown, said, "They have addicted me to narcotics, sir."

"I know. How badly?"

"Not as badly as they think."

"You need a fix now? We have a lot to do."

"I prefer immediate withdrawal."

"You might louse us up. I know where some stuff is." I was thinking of the decoy packet I delivered to Fucilla that the captain would have kept someplace in his office.

"No." His tone was adamant.

"Okay, it's your sweat, buddy."

The lieutenant said nervously, "We've been too long, señor. It would be wise to hurry."

I nodded and looked at Victor Sable. "Let's go. Stay in front of like you're being marched to an interrogation. If there's any trouble, hit the floor."

He smiled gently. "Tell me one thing, please."

"What?"

"Are you instructed to kill me if this is unsuccessful?"

I nodded.

"Good. Please don't hesitate. My death is more preferable than falling into the hands of the Reds."

"You're that big, then?"

"Exactly. I'm that big. Alive, and they somehow force me to talk, I can be responsible for the death of millions. Dead . . . well, at least it gives the world a chance to come to its senses."

"First we'll try to get you out alive," I told him.

"You're a brave man," he said.

I shook my head. "You're looking at the stupidest guy alive," I said. "Come on."

No one questioned us as we passed through the corridors. The lieutenant represented the chain of command whose word was law and the gates opened and closed behind us. In the dim light from the emergency bulbs strung along the walls, none of them could see the bulge of the gun under my coat or the note of urgency that must have been in our expressions. They simply did as they had done before, allowed the prisoner out under escort for interrogation. Later, to protect themselves and their new captain they would remember how I pressed against him as if I had a gun in his side and how he had tried to warn them silently that something was wrong, but how they, as simple guards, weren't equipped to handle such subtleties.

Only the one with the hostile eyes who had seen the world come and go, who had a hatred for all authority whose positions he coveted so badly, put up any opposition at all. In his ferretlike mind a few things fell into place and he saw the lieutenant in a gross error that could reduce him to nothingness while he elevated himself, and he whipped the pistol from the topless holster and pointed it through the bars of the gate.

His mistake was thinking the lieutenant was in charge. I shot him through his smile, watched him rebound off the desk and collapse in a heap in front of us. Without a word the lieutenant snaked his hand through the bars, recovered his keys and opened the door. Victor Sable gave me an odd look, then went through in front of us.

The others had heard the shot. They came running around the opposite end of the corridor as we were walking up it, guns drawn, then saw us approaching and stopped. They looked at each other, waiting for somebody to make a move, then glanced back at the lieutenant.

I spoke in their own language to make sure they understood. "An accident. The lieutenant had told him not to cut the top from his holster. When he dropped his keys and bent down to retrieve them the gun fell and went off."

Apparently the dead guard had stated his views on locked holstered guns too often. The explanation was enough. Their relieved grins broke the tension as they thought about the ribbing they were going to be able to give the smart old campaigner who always treated them like the idiots they were, secretly enjoying the chewing out they figured the lieutenant must have given him.

We were passed through the last gate and behind us everything became quiet and routine again, only our feet making hollow, echoing sounds on the flagstones as we walked toward the office.

But Lady Luck who had been so generous up to now decided to get a little waspish. The startled shout behind us echoed off the walls and was picked up by others. One of those guards who hadn't been able to wait to stick the needle into the one who had dropped his gun had gone back and found him dead.

I grabbed the lieutenant by his arm. "How many up ahead?"

"About thirty at various stations, señor."

"Can they be alerted?"

The lieutenant held up his hand for quiet. In back of us the excited shouts had quieted and we knew they were trying to work out a course of action. The only thing that was holding them back for the moment was that the lieutenant still represented authority and the responsibility was his. To them, he hadn't been under a gun and what he had pleased to tell them was his own affair. It wouldn't take long for them to put the pieces together and investigate even further back to the initial guard, and when they found him out cold all hell would break loose.

The lieutenant understood it as well as I did. He said, "If they hit the alarm it will bring the others inside to their stations. They will converge on us from all sides. There are standing orders as to what they should do then." He gave me a hopeless shrug.

"Is the alarm system connected to the lights?"

He shook his head. "No. It is separate wiring."

I knew where I was and knew what I had to do. I gave a quick jerk of my head for them to follow me and started off at a half trot to the corridor that bisected the one we were in. I was working against minutes and seconds now and each one that passed brought us closer to the deadline.

When I reached the turn I cut right, found the beams that framed the slab leading to the floor below and yanked out the bolts Fucilla had so nicely showed me, and pushed against the granite block. The lieutenant watched with amazement, wondering at my intimate knowledge of the secret mechanics of the fortification, a new respect in his face.

Unasked, he reached in his belt and handed me a small flashlight. I had no choice but to trust him. If he decided to play it against me it was lost and if I took the time to herd him and Sable through the maze below we'd run out of time and that would end it too.

I took the flashlight and handed him my .45. "Wait
here," I said.

The few bulbs that were strung at odd intervals were
enough to show me the way. I wasn't on any grand tour
this time and could bypass all the grisly exhibits that furnished the row of rooms. I skirted around the gory reminders of the Rose Castle's past and probable present,
the *thump-thump* of the gasoline engine like a pathfinder
signal up ahead.

This time I didn't have to bother picking a lock. The
door stayed shut under an old-fashioned thumb latch and
pulled open with squeaking reluctance when I yanked on
the handle. I flashed the beam of the light on the antique
two-cylinder marine engine pounding away slowly, throwing its power through a gear system that eventually spun
the aged generator far below its maximum capacity, spotted the plugs that fired it and yanked them loose with a
little shower of sparks and a relieved groan from the massive flywheel as it gradually came to a halt.

Behind me the dim light of the bulbs faded into total
darkness and only the small shaft of the flashlight was left
to pick my way out. But it was enough. The shadows were
grimmer and deeper, the implements of human agony
more grotesque than before, almost coming alive as the
light wove through them, their shadows reaching out for
me.

I found the stairs, went up them quickly, hit the activat-
ing lever and pulled the massive slab open.

The shot went off in front of my face as I dived and
rolled across the corridor, cursing under my breath. The
flash skittered across the floor, still on, and in its beam I
could see the guard at the intersection of the corridor
down, squirming on his rifle, his low moan still smothered
in the reverberating roar of the .45.

A hand yanked me to my feet and the lieutenant said,
"It was necessary, señor." I grabbed the flashlight, scram-
bled to my feet and played the light over Victor Sable and
the lieutenant. He was holding the gun out to me. "There
will be others coming, señor. We must hurry."

"They find the alarm?"

"You were in time," he said.

They weren't the smartest in the world, but they knew a
few basic maneuvers. I deliberately let them see the light
from the flash leading our way. When we reached the intersection I let it cover the avenues leading away, settled
on one as if we were going to take it, then rolled the light

across the floor, the beam pointing in the opposite direction.

All of them were lined up in a nice neat row, their rifles at their shoulders, waiting for us to be silhouetted against the light. Only now they were the targets and in the two seconds of confusion before they realized their position, the .45 went off under my fist and each time it bucked, one went down. The last triggered off a single shot and was reaching for the bolt on the rifle to reload when my slug caught him in the chest and he jerked and sagged under the impact, going down like a puppet whose strings were cut. When the echoes of the blast died way I picked up the light, made sure the corridor was cleared and glanced at the lieutenant.

"Could they have heard us?"

"No, señor. If they did, they will not investigate. This is not their affair. They will wait for further orders."

"Then let's go," I said. "We have to get to the office."

Nobody had touched the bodies. They lay where they fell, still outraged in their death positions, the surprise obliterated from their faces. Sable looked at them without any show of emotion, knowing that it was all part of what had to happen. They had dealt out death themselves and then suddenly it was their turn, and for that type there was no remorse.

The lieutenant reached up, clawed his jacket open, popping the buttons to the floor, then tore one lapel loose. He ran his fingers through his carefully combed hair so that it hung down over his eyes, then deliberately ripped two of his medals off, pulling part of the cloth with it and tossed them on the floor.

I knew what he was getting ready for and grinned, but before he could go into the rest of the act the phone rang. In the unnatural stillness it was a jarring note and the lieutenant reached for it automatically. His voice was crisp and official-sounding. He said *"Sí"* twice, listened carefully, then thanked the caller and hung up.

When he turned around he said, "That was my brother who works at the switchboard in Señor Ortega's office. He and Director Sabin are on the way here with three cars of armed guards."

"Did he say why?"

"*Sí*, Señor. Something about Carlos Ortega receiving a radio communication from his agent in Miami. They have suspected what is happening tonight."

I pointed to the phone. "That a straight line?"

"Correct, señor."

I walked around the desk, dialed the number of the hotel and asked for Angelo in Spanish. This time they would be monitoring all the calls for anyone speaking English and the probability would be they'd ignore the others.

When I got him I went into a jabber of small talk about women without letting him get a word in edgewise to get any other ears off the line, then said, "The boat that José could not keep and has already left . . . you remember that one?"

He recognized me immediately then. *"Sí,* it was too bad, señor."

"What port will he hit?"

"Weather advisory says the storm will head for the Florida Keys after passing over us. Miami, naturally, will be his destination."

"Direct route?"

"The only logical way, señor. He will barely have time to make it."

"See if you can raise him by radio. Tell him to look for pennies from heaven."

"Señor . . . ?"

"He'll know what I mean. I hope." I paused and said, "Thanks, kid," before I hung up.

And now it was *almost* done.

With a grand gesture that nobody else could imitate, the lieutenant clicked his heels together, saluted me smartly and snapped his hand to his side.

"I am ready, señor." He flashed me a quick smile. "If you don't mind, perhaps a small scar? The ladies . . . well . . ."

"Just one thing more."

"What is that, señor?"

"There may be a change in administrations in this country before long. If you are in any position of influence, use it wisely. One of us might come back again."

"I am aware of that possibility, señor," he replied. "Now, the scar . . . just a small one?"

I hit him before he finished talking and he was going to have his small scar. The blood would be all over the place and there would be no denying what had happened. He'd have a sore face and one hell of a black eye for a couple of weeks and he'd be a hero. If he stayed smart he'd stay a live hero and the chances were that he would. He lay on the floor in a scarlet heap close to his former captain, luckier by far than he.

The dead commander still had the two-ounce packet of H on him and I dumped it in the inkwell on the desk. I broke the glass of the gun cabinet on the wall, yanked a bayonet from an antique rifle and pried open the lock on the sliding doors of the cabinet beneath it and found the rest of the arsenal nestling in neat compartments. I grabbed four grenades, hung them on my belt and nodded for Victor Sable to follow me out.

It was five minutes after four and in the east the sun was working its way up the other side of the earth.

Now I was glad Frances was hanging out there offshore in all her awesome power. I was glad the electricity from the city was cut off to make them rely on an inadequate generator. The pair guarding the main gate couldn't make us out in the darkness and waited until I was right on top of them before the challenge came. The captain had told them to admit me, but that I wouldn't be leaving; and my appearing out of the darkness was too much of a surprise. They hesitated long enough to want to call in for instructions and when the one turned his back I cold-cocked him with the .45 and as the other brought the rifle up I let him have one in the mouth that separated him from his gun and sent him spinning into the steel grillework. He had been moving when I hit him, so he was only dazed and had the instincts of a cat. He was on his feet as I moved in, his hand going for the short knife at his belt.

I didn't have time to play the blade instead of the man and give him the chance to shout an alarm, so I took the first thrust in a quick sidestep and felt it go diagonally across my ribs like the touch of a brand. He never got the second chance. I had his arm pinioned, snapped it at the joint and crippled him with a knee in the testicles that sucked the air out of his lungs with a high whine. The butt end of the .45 wiped all the pain away instantly and left him twitching on the stone floor in unconscious reflex.

The power was out, so there wouldn't be any use trying to activate the gate. The only thing I could hope for was a manual emergency device and I flicked the light around to find it. A packing crate the guards had been using for a table concealed it, but when I kicked it away I saw the hand-operated winch there and leaned my weight against the handle and started it turning. I had to break through the rust before it began to draw against the cables and haul the gate up. With the spiked ends only four feet off the ground something jammed and it wouldn't go any farther. I waved Victor Sable under it and felt for the arm that would keep the winch from unwinding. What was there was a broken chunk of metal that wouldn't reach the gears. For some stupid reason I laughed. It wasn't the time or place, but I laughed. Lady Luck wasn't giving me any chance at all anymore. All I could hope for was that the same rust that held back the action getting the gate up would slow it coming down . . . only this time the sheer weight of the gate itself would be working against me. One chance. That was all I had. I let go the lever, made a flying dive under the grillework and lay there sweating on the ground just before the lancelike tips slid into their slots.

Sable reached down and helped me to my feet. I felt for the grenades on my belt and checked the .45, then put it away, the metal a warm friend against my side. He looked at his hand and wiped it on his coat. "You're hurt."

"I've been hurt before."

"You may need attention."

"Later," I said. "There isn't time now." I pulled him toward the Volvo, waited until he was in and turned the key in the ignition. All I could think of was, *Damn, it may work yet!*

Holding the speed down was almost painful, but to rush would be fatal. The headlights picked up the two guards on patrol who flanked the road, their rifles ready. I tapped the low-beam switch to get the light out of their eyes and leaned out of the window and called them over. I held up two of the bills I flicked from my pocket and said, "The captain told me to give you this and that he appreciated your services."

The denomination was too much for them. One even rested his rifle up against a tree to inspect the bill in the glare of the lights and the hardest part was keeping them from shaking my hand in gratitude. Anybody else would have pocketed the money and to hell with them. The one on the barricade that led to the road was a little more suspicious until I chewed him out enough to take the money out of my hand; then he was all smiles and bewilderment, but shrewd enough to know what that single bill represented in his present economy.

When we were clear, Sable turned to me with a slight smile and said, "Does your country always prepare you so well for an emergency?"

"This was my own idea. Nothing motivates the impoverished more than the sight of riches."

"You are difficult to understand, my friend. I wonder what motivates you."

"Sometimes I wonder myself," I said. "For the time being, call me a sucker."

"I don't believe that."

"What do you think, then?"

"Most likely I could tell you, but most likely you wouldn't accept it either."

"And that I appreciate," I said.

I saw their headlights bouncing off the treetops in the distance, the glow diffused by the low night clouds overhead. I touched the brake pedal and skidded to a stop before I reached the curve in the road, slammed the Volvo into reverse and sent it smashing into the bushes off the shoulder, angling it toward the oncoming cars so their lights wouldn't pick up any reflection from the glass in ours. I told Sable to stay put until I got back, then climbed out my side and ran back the way we had come about fifty yards, picked my spot and waited.

Leaders never lead anymore. They send their troops out ahead to pick up any itinerant fire and stay safe on the excuse that their services are too valuable to be exposed to enemy destruction. I pulled the pins from two of the grenades and held the handles down under my fingers, judging the speed of the oncoming column. A hundred feet separated each of the vehicles and I let the first two trucks loaded with soldiers roll past, released the handle of a grenade and heard it pop into life, then let it go with an overhand swing into the path of the command car in the rear.

I was off on my timing, but I wasn't off on my aim. The grenade, momentarily lost in the darkness, slashed through the beams of the headlights and wiped out the windshield with its crashing impact as the vehicle swerved wildly when the driver reacted to his surprise. But he tried too hard and overcontrolled and the car whipped around, hit the soft shoulders of the road and toppled slowly and ponderously on its side.

The damn fuse had a longer delay than I anticipated and they almost had time to get out. The door opened upward, the interior light winking on so I could see both Carlos Ortega and Russo Sabin fighting madly for escape. Only the driver had guts enough to scream, "Grenade, grenade!" and scrabble for it someplace in the car.

Then it blew and Ortega and Sabin were lifted in disjointed pieces from the wreckage and scattered through the night with a lovely orange blossom of flame to send them off with a final salute.

Up ahead the other trucks had stopped and had started backing up. I let the other grenade go rolling down the road and ran like hell back toward the car. I barely reached the Volvo when it went off and I didn't bother to check the damage it did. Those troops would be scrambling for cover, waiting for another attack, and weren't going to be watching for me driving off in the dark.

I felt my way along the road, turned on the dims when I rounded the turn, having barely enough light to see the road. When I was far enough away I switched on the low beams, hit the gas pedal and headed toward the highway.

Only then did I have a chance to notice Victor Sable in the seat beside me. He looked like he was frozen there, his face pale and drawn. "Relax," I said.

The sound of my voice seemed to startled him back to reality. "They are . . . ?"

"Dead," I told him. I glanced in the rear-view mirror. We were still alone on the road. I looked at my watch and grinned to myself. We just might make it at that.

Sable's hands were folded into tight knots in his lap. "This killing," he said. "All this terrible killing . . ."

"Save your sympathy," I told him. "That's how they got on top."

The Volvo careened around a curve, straightened and slowed as the intersection I was looking for came up. Ortega might have given orders to have roadblocks set up on the highway and I didn't want to take any chances of running into them. The back route I had taken to the Rose Castle was longer, but less likely to be patrolled. I swung onto the dirt road and tramped on the throttle again.

Ahead of us the revolving beacon of the airfield still probed the sky with its finger of light and I was sure of my direction. I was pushing for time and almost pushed myself into the wreckage of the trap that I had laid myself.

Sable saw it the same time I did, let out a hoarse yell and was reaching for the wheel when I batted his arm away. Right in the center of the road an old Chevvy that had been parked next to the Volvo in the hotel lot was upside down in the midst of the wreckage of the cart I had dragged into its path.

I stopped, pointed the lights of the car at the mess, got out with the .45 cocked in my hand and looked inside it.

The steering wheel was bent in half and blood was flecked over the cushions and broken glass, but nobody was there. The door on the driver's side gaped open and I didn't like standing there in the light making a target of myself for anybody who still might be in the bushes, even though the chances were he had long since gone. I got back in the Volvo, skirted the wreck and stayed on the road until it bent around the perimeter of the airfield.

From there it was a straight run to the north end and I cut the lights, letting the occasional glow from the beacon spot my way as I lined up on the windows in the tower a mile away. The wind was at our backs now, whistling past the window in furious gusts that rocked the car. Hurricane Frances was getting her back up, ready to move in for the kill.

The beacon light swept by again and this time outlined a dark bulk in the road in time for me to slow down. A tractor had been abandoned in our path and there wasn't room to cut around it. I opened the door, shoved Sable out and followed him.

In a way it was a lucky break. There might have been a guard posted at the gate up ahead and time was too short to have to fight my way through it. The hood of the tractor provided easy access over the fence and when I dropped down I turned and caught Sable as he jumped, made sure he was all right and got on the macadam taxi strip.

What planes hadn't been hangared were all choked and tied down in the grass off the runway, sitting there like frightened giants, quivering gently in the wind. Four aged DC-3's and a pair of converted B-25's with military insignia were side by side, relics of another war but still active, a symbol of the power and authority that had held the country in submission.

I told Sable to wait, ran to one of the B-25's and climbed in. I didn't have to scrounge very hard to find what I wanted. I disregarded the back packs still in the pilots' bucket seats and dug out one of the emergency chest-pack chutes and harness, stuffed it into a canvas bag that was lying in the corner and got out of there.

Sable was waiting nervously, his back to the wind, and was relieved to see me appear out of the darkness. I wanted to leave my hands free, so I handed him the bag. "Keep this," I said. "And don't lose it."

He hefted the bag curiously, wondering what it was. "Important?"

"You'll never know," I said.

In the east the cloud layers had taken on the dull glow of a false dawn, black entrails of turbulence like mean streaks rolling in its midst. I said, "Let's go," and we broke into a trot to cover the last quarter mile.

The buildings around the control tower and administration complex were all but deserted. Even the skeleton crew was taking off for the shelter of safer places. A gasoline truck moved out, its headlights picking up the gate, and I saw it stop to be inspected by uniformed guards carrying rifles and tommy guns who scanned the occupants before letting them pass on.

Whenever the beacons flashed by overhead we flattened to the ground, then got up to cover more ground between its sweeps, hoping that nobody saw us outlined against the lights of the buildings. Each time I hit the grass I tried to pick out the shape of the Queenaire against the formless jumble of shapes in the semidarkness.

And then I saw it parked at a forty-five-degree angle into the wind, at the end of the runway, and grabbed Victor Sable's arm and ran toward it. We were too close to the end of it all and I didn't smell the danger until I got that warm feeling in the small of my back again and saw Sable trip and go down. I grabbed him under the shoulder and went to haul him to his feet and almost fell over the same obstacle.

Joey Jolley was lying there, a vicious slash across his forehead, a low moan choking out of lips drawn back in pain. His eyes opened, recognized me, and his lips moved in warning, but it was too late.

A voice said, "I've been waiting for you, Morgan."

They were there in the partial shadow under the wing of an old Stinson, and Marty Steele had Kim's arm wrenched up behind her back and was holding a gun against her head.

The beacon swept by again and in its light I could see his face, cut and bloody from the wreckage of when he had smashed into the cart on the road. But the lacerations had done something else, too. They had released the tension on artifically tightened skin, put his features back into recognizable contours and I knew who he was.

I said, "Hello, Dekker. It's been a long time."

His tone was almost friendly. "It won't be much longer, Morg."

"Why'd you wait all this time for?"

I saw his grin. "I had to be sure, old buddy. I'm surprised you didn't figure it out. You're losing the old edge. You used to be the bright boy in the group."

"It finally began to figure out."

Once again the beacon light hit him and his face had a wild look of controlled insanity, the expression Bernice Case had described, filled with hatred and kill lust.

I said, "When you picked Whitey Tass off I knew it had to be you. He didn't even know you were here, but had he seen you and he could have identified you."

"You play it safe when the stakes are big enough, Morgan."

"Are they, Dekker?"

He chuckled flatly, the sound humorless and cold. "You're damn right. Forty million bucks' worth of high stakes and its's all mine. When you got nailed for the job I nearly laughed my head off. I used the same technique you taught me and you get rapped for it."

"Why, kid?"

He wasn't laughing now. "Something you idiotic patriots wouldn't understand. You didn't get blown apart by a lousy mine. You didn't get shafted by the government and stuck in a hospital to rot with a frigging little pension and some medals for thanks. You know what happened when a broad looked at my face? I saw one of them vomit once. Well, piss on that. I couldn't even stand the country. I got the hell out and saved my money until I got a new face and a new name and came back to make the good old U.S.A. pay me what I earned."

"Whose body did they bury under your name, Dekker?"

I got that chuckle again. "I've killed too many to worry about him. He was just a stupid Australian sheepherder named Marty Steele if it matters to you."

"Too bad you didn't get to spend all that dough, Sal."

"Oh, I will, old buddy. I will. I got it hidden right where your namesake, Captain Henry Morgan himself, kept his little pile and I'm the only one who can get to it." He paused a few seconds, then said, "You should have moved in quicker, Morg."

He had said all he was going to say and I saw his hand tighten around the gun he held at Kim's head. He was going to take her out first, then me, and I had to stop him. I said, "I wasn't on your back, Dekker."

Curiosity stopped his trigger finger. "Get off it, buddy."

"You knew I was on the run," I told him. "You knew Old Gussie ran a hideout spot and you should have figured my checking in there after you cut out was only accidental. It's a crazy coincidence, but it happened."

"Nothing's coincidental in this world. Don't feed me that crap."

"So a hunk of coal dust from Pennsylvania gets in your eye in New York and it's all part of a plan, is that it?"

"You showed up here," he accused.

"I was on another deal, Sal. It was nothing to do with you at all. I knew Ortega and Russo had their men on me, but they wouldn't have taken a shot at me with a .38. You know, that was the first time I ever knew you to miss one that close. I moved just in time. If you had tried for the body instead of a head shot you would have gotten me."

"You think . . ."

I cut him off, playing for seconds. "It was you outside my door that night in the hotel, you watching me all the time, you who followed me into the restaurant and saw me contact Rosa Lee. You were the only one who could have figured out the possible exits from the hotel nobody else would ever use and cover it until I came out. You're the only one who could have tailed me without being seen, Sal."

His chuckle had satisfaction in it this time.

"Why'd you bump Rosa Lee, Sal?"

Dekker's voice still tasted the pleasure of the kill. "I bought my way into this country, Morgan. Ortega and Sabin were making me pay plenty for the privilege. Any one of the natives could have been onto the pitch and ready to set me up for a hit. Don't tell me she wasn't putting you onto me."

"She wasn't."

"Save that crap for the enlisted men, Morgan," he snarled. "Bringing Tass in to pick me out wrapped it up. Hell, you never knew me. The plastic surgeons did too good a job for that, but Tass saw me after I was fixed up and could have fingered me."

"He came in to kill the guy you cold-cocked here, the one who could have fingered *him*."

"Too bad, Morgan."

"You still got to get out of here, Dekker," I reminded him. "Ortega and Russo are dead. Your cover is gone now. The ones who take over now are going to get into their records and come up with your name in the package and put the pieces together."

"That won't make any difference, old buddy. I was ready to cut out for greener fields anyway. There are three guys in that plane that came to pick you up. They're sitting there waiting and what they're going to get is me and this doll here. She was very nice about talking it out with your jumpy friend to keep him from getting the screaming meemies while they waited.

"After you dumped them out I knew what you were scheming up. I made my mistake in trying to get you and you suckered me into your roadblock. But hell, Morgan, it was a lucky mistake at that. I got back here and found my ticket out all ready and waiting."

"You bump the pilot of that plane and you're stranded, Sal."

That laugh of his was flatter than ever. "Out in the bushes of Australia the only way you get places is by air. I can fly that crate, old buddy. It's one of my newer accomplishments."

He was ready now and there was nothing more left to talk about. I said, "It was a sheer waste, Sal. All you should have done was wait me out and you would have had it all to yourself with clear running in front of you. Now you'll never make it."

The light was enough to show his face in a frenzied grin. "What makes you think so, Morgan?"

"Because you didn't come out of the war like the rest of us. What happened tipped you off balance until you hated your own country so much you were going to make it pay through the nose for what you thought it did to you. Others survived the same things, but you never considered that. All you cared about was repayment. That's why you went after government money instead of any other source."

I gave him just enough time to let it sink in and added, *"Dekker . . . you're crazy!"*

And with a scream of madness choking in his throat he made the mistake I was waiting for and yanked the gun from Kim's head, throwing the first shot at me.

I knew what was coming and was moving to the right, the .45 jumping into my hand like it had a life of its own, and when I triggered it the slug blasted his head in half, spattering Kim with a spray of gore.

Before she had time to reflect on it I had her by the arm, got Joey to his feet and Sable running ahead of us toward the plane. Behind us muffled shouts were carried on the wind and somebody sent a wild shot richocheting across the field.

They saw us coming and the twin props coughed into

motion. I got them aboard, picked the last two grenades from my belt, pulled the pins and threw them as hard as I could at the cluster of figures running toward us, triggered off the last of the rounds in the .45 in their direction and ran for the door of the plane. The hand that yanked me inside jerked the gun from my fingers, tossed it outside and slammed the door as the Queenaire swung out on the runway under full throttle and lifted off almost at once in the strong breath of Hurricane Frances.

Ten minutes out the sudden morning sun cut through the scud like a knife and we lifted to three thousand feet. The pilot hadn't had time to top his tanks before takeoff, and bucking the headwind to reach Nuevo Cádiz had depleted his gas supply to a point critical enough to give him barely a margin of safety. He picked up a direct course for Miami, grateful now for the wind at his back.

I sat next to Kim because she wanted it that way. Across the aisle Joey was holding a wet towel to his head, slumped in the window seat with Victor Sable beside him. Behind me was the third guy who came in, sitting there with a gun in his lap because Kim refused to let him shackle me the way he had wanted to.

Below us the sun was sparkling off the water. It was a nice day and in less than an hour we'd be in Miami. Kim sat there watching the day begin, her hands folded in her lap. Her fingers still held the slip of paper the guy behind me handed her, the receipt for my person. Her responsibility had ended and now I belonged to the man with the gun who had one of those bland faces of the professional who would kill if it was necessary and whom you couldn't fake out with words.

She knew I was looking at her and turned her head and smiled, impulsively reaching over for my hand. She squeezed gently and said, "I heard what he said, Morgan. I'll tell them everything, you know. They'll have to release you."

I shook my head. "You don't know your own people, baby."

Her puzzled frown was reflected in her eyes. "I . . . don't understand."

"You're a woman, my lovely wife. You're a luscious, sexy doll who's been running with a wild-assed guy and living with him legally joined in matrimony while we played the game, and women have been known to turn emotional under those conditions and forget what they came for. Right now you even got the look to go with it. In a million years, you couldn't make them believe we weren't in the sack together, and when you have your clothes off in the dark on a soft bed a woman is only a woman and a better one if she's a wife . . . and when she becomes a wife she'd do anything to save her husband. It's as simple as that, Kim."

Anger sparked her eyes open. "There's Sable and Jolley . . ."

"Joey's word would count for nothing. They'd know what he is. And nobody will be talking about Victor Sable. What happened back there never happened at all, officially. There will be rumors and speculation, but the hurricane and the new bunch taking over will confuse the whole issue and even the Reds won't be able to make any propaganda out of it.

"No, baby, they won't talk about it and won't believe you and the only item that could turn the trick would be if Sal Dekker had told us where he planted all that beautiful money."

For a moment she just stared at me, her eyes shiny with a wet film that welled into twin teardrops in their corners. "But he did, Morgan."

This time I didn't understand.

She said, "Where your namesake hid his riches."

"They never found that, either."

"Maybe they never tried hard enough."

I felt all the little hairs on my arms raise up and a tiny prickling sensation eat at my skin. I leaned back against the seat and said, "You know, maybe it would have been pretty damn good at that."

"What, Morgan?"

"Suppose I could have been cleared? Suppose we had that forty million to turn in and they had to listen to you and take Joey and Sable's word for it." I turned my head and looked at her. "What would you do about it now?"

Her smile was wry and she wiped the tears out of her eyes. "Nothing," she said. "I wouldn't have to. We're already married."

"You mean I wouldn't have to rape you?"

The smile laughed at me gently and her face was a glorious thing, dirty but beautiful; hair mussed but lovely, those full breasts pouting against the restraint of her clothes and the hem of the dress hiked up comfortably over full round thighs that were too exciting to look at long. "You might call it that," she said, "but I'd help you."

My hand squeezed hers. "I love you, Kim."

The gentle pressure of her fingers said the same as her words. "I love you, Morgan the Raider."

"I'm thinking again," I said.

"I know you are," she told me.

"They don't call me the Raider for nothing, you know."

"Naturally not."

I looked at my watch and leaned over to scan the water below.

"It might take a while, but you'll have to wait for me."

She didn't even know what I was thinking, but whatever it was satisfied her completely. "Forever if I have to."

"Nobody else?"

"They'd *really* have to rape me."

"It's going to be fun," I said.

"The best."

"See you," I said, and saw the confidence behind the puzzle in her eyes.

I raked my nails across the cut I had gotten from the knife of the guard back at the Rose Castle and started the blood running down my side again. I pulled my shirt away so they could see it wasn't a phony and winced loudly enough so Sable turned and looked at me. I caught his eyes, hoped my expression conveyed what I wanted when I let them focus on the canvas bag he had at his feet, the one I made him carry, then stood up with my shirt back so the guy behind me could see what had happened.

"This thing's bugging me, feller. Mind if I go back there and clean it up?"

He had the gun pointed at my head, but one look at the raw, open wound wiped any suspicion out of his face. I was his responsibility now and he wanted me delivered whole and healthy. He started to get up to go to the lavatory with me, and Victor Sable got into the act.

He picked up the bag, held up his hand and said, "Please, I am a doctor, among other things. Perhaps I can be of assistance."

The guy frowned, nodded and sat back, but turned in his seat to watch us all the way.

Time and distance overlapped, that of the plane coinciding with that of the boat that was a small dot on the face of the sea below. We came out of the tiny lavatory with Sable leading the way so that he blocked the view of me in the chest pack, and when the guy did finally see it Victor Sable stumbled deliberately into him, smothering his gun hand with his clumsiness as I reached for the handle on the door of the plane and forced it open.

I had a wad of loot in my pocket to do what I had to do and if the guy in the boat was able to reach me he'd know what pennies from heaven really mean.

There was a happy glow in Kim's eyes and a laugh on her mouth and words that said, *"Go, husband!"* as she made a *V* with two fingers, crossed it with her other forefinger to make the sign of the delta factor, then pointed to herself so I'd remember that she was the only delta left for me.

I couldn't hold back the wild laugh and it must have been just like Old Henry himself let out when he mocked the whole world.

Then I jumped.